'So that's how it's gonna be.'

Nick took three long strides, opened the freezer door and wriggled out several ice cubes from the plastic bag.

Ryanne squealed and ran out the back door before he turned around. He gave chase, the door slamming behind him. This was a game they'd played hundreds of times as kids. She'd been taller, longer-legged and had escaped. But this time his legs were the longer ones and he caught up to her as she tried to open the front door.

Flattening a palm against the wood, he trapped her in the prison formed by his body.

Her eyes were wide, revealing her perplexity. A pulse beat at the base of her throat and her feminine scent rose up to envelop him. She lowered her gaze to his lips for a heated second.

'You don't play fair,' she said to him, the anger missing from her tone.

He lowered his head and kissed her...

Available in July 2003 from Silhouette Special Edition

Nick All Night
CHERYL ST. JOHN

SILHOUETTE®
SPECIAL EDITION™

*First published in Great Britain 2003
Silhouette Books, Eton House, 18-24 Paradise Road,
Richmond, Surrey TW9 1SR*

© Cheryl Ludwigs 2002

ISBN 0 373 24475 4

23-0703

*Printed and bound in Spain
by Litografia Rosés S.A., Barcelona*

CHERYL ST. JOHN

A peacemaker, a romantic, an idealist and a discouraged perfectionist are the words that Cheryl St. John uses to describe herself. Cheryl, an author of both historical and contemporary novels, says she's been told that she is painfully honest.

Cheryl admits to being an avid collector who collects everything from dolls to Depression glass, brass candlesticks, old photographs and, most especially, books. She and her husband love to browse antique and collectible shops.

She says that knowing her stories bring hope and pleasure to readers is one of the best parts of being a writer. Another wonderful part is being able to set her own schedule and have time to work around her growing family.

Cheryl loves to hear from readers. You can write to her at: PO Box 12142, Florence Station, Omaha, NE 68112, USA, or at SaintJohn@aol.com

Chapter One

Nick Sinclair drew a breath, edged his back along the wall and, without making a sound, spun into the bedroom with his Smith and Wesson double-action automatic steadied in both hands. "Freeze!"

The resulting scream startled him so badly he almost dropped the gun, but he stared determinedly down the barrel at the room's sole occupant.

A curvaceous blonde in a tiny ribbed undershirt thing that didn't even cover her belly button, and a pair of silky white bikini panties, had dropped the stack of clothing she'd been moving, and spun around to stare at him.

From the cheap old plastic stereo on the maple dresser, the Rolling Stones sang about not getting any satisfaction—words with which Nick sorely identified.

My God, she had the tiniest waist and the longest, sexiest legs he'd ever seen. Beneath that useless shirt, he could see round little breasts and perky nipples as plain as day. Her hair had been tied up on her head and a riotous jumble of curls fell to one side of her face. She stared at him with terrified, wide blue eyes. *Ryanne Whitaker's eyes.*

Ryanne had lived in California for years now, since high school, and her mother, who still owned this home, had a place in Arizona. At the unexpected lights and the music, he'd assumed kids had broken into the house next door to his. He lowered the gun. "Ryanne?"

Her expression changed perceptibly, a flicker of concern replacing the fear, but puzzlement evident. "Nick?" she said, finally recognizing him. "What are you doing here?"

"Hell, Ryanne, I thought someone had broken in. Your mom always calls me before she gets here."

Immediately, her expression and her tone became angry. "'*What* are you doing here?' I asked. How did you get in?"

"I have a key."

"My mom gave you a key?"

He nodded. "I take care of things for her, check the pipes and turn on the heat or the air-conditioning before she arrives."

"So you just come on in and nose around whenever you feel like it?"

"No! I thought you were a burglar. There aren't many burglaries in Elmwood, but lately teens have been breaking into empty houses to party."

"Thus the whole 'freeze' routine," she commented dryly.

God, she'd always been able to make him feel stupid. Like a freshman caught with his zipper down in the school cafeteria. "If I'd known it was you, I wouldn't have been concerned."

"I wasn't aware that I needed to report in with my whereabouts. Neither did I think it was illegal to put my own underwear in my own dresser drawers."

He'd heard the slamming of drawers from downstairs and had imagined someone ransacking the place. He tried unsuccessfully to look at the underwear in her hands, rather than the panties she was wearing.

"Unless," she added, "Elmwood has passed some new lingerie ordinance since I've been gone."

They should have, he thought with an uncomfortable twinge, because this eyeful had to be illegal. All that satiny-looking skin, the miniscule triangle of silk... Stupid wasn't the only way she'd made him feel. "Are...um...you alone here?"

He knew from Evelyn that Ryanne was married, but her husband never seemed to accompany her on trips home. Still, the guy could be here somewhere. The *lucky* guy.

Seeing the direction of his gaze, she grabbed up a silky gown from the bed and held it in front of her knockout body. "No accomplices along this time. Just me."

"Where's your husband?"

She stiffened and gave him a frown. "Look, Magnum. Now that you've seen I'm not hiding the silver in my pockets, you can be on your way."

Nick glanced down at his short-sleeved khaki uniform shirt and trousers. He'd thought twice about strapping on his holster before heading over, but the kids always did a double take when they saw his gun, and took him seriously when he wore it. Part of the persona. Part of his duty. He'd figured if he ran into a houseful of teens looking for trouble, they wouldn't have known he hadn't loaded it.

He slid the automatic into its sheath and snapped the closure. She hadn't answered his question. "What are you doing here?"

Ryanne hadn't been back in Elmwood more than half a dozen times in all the years since she'd left. And those times had been over holidays.

"This is still my mother's home. I don't need to explain to you why I'm here."

"No, you don't have to. I was just…curious."

She flicked her fingers in a dismissing motion toward the hallway. "You know what they say about curiosity."

He backed out and she followed, giving him another eyeful as she moved the robe to shrug into it. Ironically, he'd been lamenting his sexual frustration only an hour ago, standing in his room, looking out into the night. A single father in a small town didn't have many opportunities for a discreet means of correcting that problem. He would never sleep tonight.

She tugged the tie into place at her waist, but the memory of what was beneath that thin layer of shimmery fabric was not forgotten. Would probably never be forgotten as long as he drew breath. He turned away from her and headed down the stairs, this time letting his weight distress the aged wood.

"I'm sure you cops on the night shift have a list of other unsuspecting woman to scare senseless tonight. Don't let me keep you."

The house looked as it had for the thirty or so years he could remember—same collection of photographs down the stairway wall, same antique furnishings, same lace curtains. He reached the door. "Actually, I'm off duty."

"We-ell," she said, as though impressed. "I'll bet you're a real ball of fire during your shift."

He had opened the door, but he turned back to face her. "Look, Rye." He used the nickname easily, and her eyes reflected her surprise. "I saw lights on over here. I checked the perimeter of the house, tested the windows and doors. I heard the music and I had a key, so I walked in. It was neighborly. It was cautious. It's also my job. So, I caught you in your underwear. Get over it."

"I'm over it."

"Good."

"Good night."

"Good night."

She slammed the door, and he heard the chain guard slide into place.

Ungrateful, irritable, *irritating* woman. There'd been a time when they'd been close, like brother and sister. More brotherly and sisterly than he'd preferred, but comfortable. Friends... But she'd been in an all-fired hurry to make something of herself and get out of Elmwood. She'd earned a business scholarship to Stanford and had never looked back.

That's why her presence here when her mother wasn't in town was puzzling. If she'd been visiting, she'd have gone to see her mom in Arizona. The boxes he'd seen in the dining room had been more than suitcases packed for a week's stay. They'd looked more like someone was moving—in.

Ryanne stood staring at the cartons in the dining room, wondering if she had the stamina to carry one more load up the stairs. Ever since packing them in California and setting out, she'd been thinking that these were pitiful few possessions to represent her entire life to this point. But this was it—all that was left, anyway, after she'd sold nearly everything to pacify the IRS.

If she'd had anywhere else to go, she would have. But this was it. The only place she knew where she could live rent-free while she tried to piece her life back together and find a job. And already it had started.

She'd been prepared for the gossipy, judgmental, holier-than-thou citizens in this town. But Nick, of all people, had already poked his nose into her business!

Nick Sinclair, the sheriff. She guessed she'd known that before, but she'd never seen him in his official capacity, never seen him in more than passing in all these years. Well, he was a man now, she admitted, a nice-looking man. Okay, he was a hunk, with that black hair and those dark brooding eyes, lips that could turn a woman inside out for wondering what they'd feel like against her skin.

Ryanne caught herself with a jolt. What a shocking thought to have about Nick, of all people! She'd been driving too long, cramped in her car, sleeping in what stingy space had not been taken up with her belongings. Isolation and tiny places could make a person crack.

Self-pitying tears smarted her eyelids, and she rubbed her eyes hastily. Who would think that she, Ryanne Davidson, would be reduced to sleeping in a car? To fitting her belongings into a vehicle and driving the whole miserable distance to her mother's home, the same place Ryanne had worked her whole life to get away from? She'd told her mother that she was coming here for a while, but she hadn't told her all the gory details. Admitting her failure out loud would take more fortitude than she had right now.

Angrily, she hefted a box and headed for the stairs. Nobody was going to find out about her humiliation; she would make certain of that. If anyone found out that her hotshot, unfaithful ex-husband had stolen funds from the company they'd started together and then disappeared, she'd be the laughingstock of the county.

She set the box beside the bed, turned off the light and stared out the window. She hadn't learned until after Mason was gone that he'd never paid taxes. Accounting had been his job in their advertising agency. Hers had been clients, new accounts and personnel. If she'd even suspected his deceit, she might have saved herself some of this grief. But she'd had no reason to question that anything was less than perfect.

They'd been making money—a lot of money. Their reputation had spread and she'd lured some top accounts under their prestigious umbrella. She and Mason had always been better at business than at marriage. When she'd learned of his numerous affairs, she hadn't been devastated, strangely enough. Mad, embarrassed, but not devastated. They'd continued a tense working relationship, but eventually she'd divorced him.

After that, he'd cashed company checks and disappeared. Ryanne had spent money she didn't have to have him traced, but to no avail. Investigators believed he'd left the country and their hands were tied. The divorce had gone through uncontested. And then the IRS had come searching.

Ryanne stared into the darkness, noting the familiar silhouette of the house next door. There was a porch on the back that hadn't been there before, and the double garage was new. As a girl, she'd stared out this window a multitude of times, wishing on stars, wondering about the world outside Elmwood and waiting for her chance to stamp her presence upon it.

Well, she'd done it, all right. A big rubber stamp that declared Loser across her forehead. She opened the window wider to allow more air into the warm, humid room. The curtains blew inward, raising the smell of dust. If she was going to be living here for a while, she'd wash them and get the place clean. Who knew how long it would be before she found a job that would pay for the debt she'd been left with?

The government hadn't been able to find Mason, either. And that left only her. She had three months before the IRS added penalties and interest that would more than double the original tax debt. She'd already liquidated the business, sold her client list, her condo…most of her jewelry. Everything but her car. A person needed transportation to find a new home and a new job.

The ever-present sense of loss, the weight of failure

pressed down on her, more oppressive than the temperature. Why had she ended up here in Iowa, of all places? A hundred times during the drive from the coast, she'd come so close to turning off, to finding a place where no one knew her, and starting over. But how? And with what? Under an assumed identity? How did a person get a driver's license and social security number in a new name? That was undoubtedly a federal offense, and she was in enough trouble. And anything done legally would bring the authorities looking for her no matter where she went.

She wasn't Mason. She couldn't turn her back on her obligations. She couldn't do something criminal to escape her stupidity in trusting him. Nor could she spend her life looking over her shoulder, wondering when the feds were going to catch up with her.

So she'd continued on, seeking somewhere to lick her wounds and regroup. The last place she wanted to be was the only place available. So here she was. But she didn't have to like it. And she didn't have to be neighborly. Even if her neighbor was Nick and she'd treated him badly without good cause. As soon as she found a job, she was out of here.

On to somewhere better.

Ryanne pulled off the chenille bedspread and lay on the cotton sheets of her old bed. Somewhere better. How many times had she lain here and thought those same thoughts? Nothing like fate biting you in the butt to bring your life full circle, was there? Had she really been that rude to someone who had only meant well? Exhausted, physically and emotionally, she fell asleep.

* * *

"There's a pretty lady over there, Dad," seven-year-old Jamie said from his padded seat in the breakfast alcove.

Nick turned with a spatula in his hand and glanced briefly out the window above the café curtains. "That's Mrs. Whitaker's daughter," he said, and went back to cooking their Saturday morning breakfast. "The one I told you about, who grew up with me and your uncle Justin."

"Ryanne's home?" Nick's father, Mel, asked, coming from the room off the kitchen, which they'd converted to his private quarters. Moving to the table and peering out the window, he emitted a long low whistle.

"Dad!" Nick said in surprise. "Little pitchers?"

"Will you look at those curves?" his father continued.

"Wow!" Jamie had joined him in making appreciative noises. "Can I go over there and look up close?"

"No!" Nick said emphatically, and turned off the fire under the skillets. He took plates from the cupboard. "Dad, will you use some decorum here?"

"What are you talking about?" Mel asked, still transfixed with the sight next door.

"I'm talking about you o-g-l-i-n-g the scenery in front of you-know-who."

Finally, his father turned his attention to Nick. "I'm surprised you're not the one over here ogling. No, I'm surprised you're not out the door and across the yard and over there running your hands over the 'scenery.'"

Shocked for real now, Nick gaped at his dad. What

had come over the old man? "What are you talking about?"

"I'm talking about the car. What are you talking about?"

"I'm talking about—the car?" He looked again. This time, his chin dropped.

Ryanne was indeed in her driveway, in a pair of short cutoffs that looked like some she must have found in her old room. After last night's enlightenment, the way she filled them out was no surprise. The surprise was the shiny red Dodge Viper glistening in the sunlight in her driveway. She lovingly washed a gleaming fender and chrome wheel with a sponge she wrung out over a dented metal bucket.

"A Viper," Nick said, his voice flat with amazement.

"Ain't she the coolest, Dad? Can I go over there, *pu-leese?*"

Ryanne happened to straighten and glance over at precisely that moment. Mel was holding back the curtain and the three of them were gaping out the window like they'd never seen a car before. Well, they hadn't, not one like that, anyway. As though realizing as one that they'd just been caught staring, the three of them pulled back. Mel let the curtain fall into place.

"No," Nick told Jamie, still holding the plates. "Let's not bother her."

"That's not neighborly," Mel protested. "Maybe we should invite her to breakfast. It's *Ryanne,* for heaven's sake." He headed for the back door.

"Dad. No, Dad."

But his father was out the door and across the porch before Nick could say more.

"Grampa's going? Now can I go over?"

Nick conceded and waved Jamie off. He placed the three plates on the table and proceeded to dish bacon, eggs and pancakes onto his own. She wouldn't be over. He'd already learned how unfriendly she'd become.

He smeared butter and poured syrup on his stack of pancakes and determinedly settled in for his meal. He had eaten several bites before he broke down and looked out the window.

She was showing them the engine.

Damn, he'd love to look under that hood, hear the motor run. Maybe if he raised the window, he could catch the sound. Nah. Probably not from this distance. That baby probably purred like a kitten. He turned determinedly back to his pancakes.

Ryanne swiped the enormous sponge over the grill, scrubbing hard at the layer of insects that had committed suicide between here and the coast. Her car had never been this dirty. She wrinkled her nose at the mess and directed the hose to rinse away the worst. The morning sun combined with her exertions to make a trickle of sweat run between her breasts under her shirt. She sprayed cold water on her legs and feet, enjoying the refreshing chill.

"I didn't know you were home!" The voice from behind surprised her, and she turned to see a gray-haired man and a young boy approaching from the Sinclair house. *Home?* The word sounded strange. "When did you get here?"

"Mel. Mel Sinclair!" Oh, my gosh, Ryanne thought. He'd aged since she'd last seen him. How long had it been? "I got here just yesterday," she replied, smiling.

"This is my grandson, Jamie. Jamie, this is Ryanne Whitaker. Oh, it's not Whitaker anymore, is it?" Mel gave her a sheepish look.

"That's okay. It's Davidson."

The dark-haired boy waved to acknowledge the introduction, but his attention was focused on the car behind her. "Wow," he said. "That's an awesome car."

A grandson. Since Mel had only one son left, the boy had to belong to Nick. She looked the handsome young fellow over, recognizing the deep-set blue eyes, the thick black hair. That cleft in his chin wasn't Nick's, however. Other than that, looking at the boy was like going back twenty-odd years and looking at Nick.

"Thanks. Are you visiting your grandfather today?" she asked to make conversation.

He brought his gaze from the car to her, then shot it to Mel.

"Jamie lives with me. With us. We live together."

"Oh." She hadn't kept up on the Sinclairs, though surely her mother had mentioned them. Ryanne remembered the news about Nick's wedding, years ago. He'd married the girl that his brother, Justin, had dated in high school. She'd thought it odd at the time, but then she hadn't been around to see a new romance blossom. What was her name? Haley? Hattie? Something like that.

"She's so cool," Jamie said, back to staring at the

car. He walked around the front, Mel following, then stood on tiptoe and peered through the driver's side window. "Bet she purrs like a kitten."

Ryanne couldn't help a smile. She exchanged a look with Mel. "Sounds just like someone else I used to know."

"He's his father's son, through and through, no gettin' around that."

"Would you like to look under the hood?" she asked, knowing that looking at engines was a guy thing.

"Cool!" was his reply.

She opened the door and popped the latch. Walking to the front of the car, she found the lever and raised the hood.

Both Mel and Jamie stared reverently. "Awesome," Jamie whispered, as though he were in church. "Dad's gonna be sorry he missed this," he said, turning to look up at her, finally giving her more attention than the car. "Are you and my dad still friends?"

She thought about the scene last night, when Nick had crashed into her bedroom and waved a gun in her face. Okay, so he'd been looking out for the house— for her mother's property—and doing what he thought should be done. Ryanne had had a really bad week, a really bad several months, actually—well, maybe more like a year—and she hadn't been in any mood to be stormed by the local sheriff on a SWAT mission.

Nick was an old friend and she hadn't been very nice, even though she'd had cause for taking offense.

"We grew up together," she said now. "Best buddies."

"I know," Jamie stated. "My dad told me." His face lit with enthusiasm, and he turned to his grandfather. "Can she come eat breakfast with us, Grampa? Dad always makes plenty."

"Oh, I wouldn't want to impose on your family...." she began.

"You are part of our family," Mel said earnestly. "Why, you used to be at our table as often as my boys. And if you weren't, then they were over here eating your mama's cooking." He gave her a smile that deepened the wrinkles around his kind eyes. "Come share breakfast with us. Please."

Ryanne didn't especially want to see Nick or his wife. Did they have other children besides Jamie? But neither did she want to hurt Mel's feelings. He'd been so good to her after her father had left. He and Nick both. And apparently Nick watched over the house for her. "All right. Just for a little while."

"Great!" Jamie shouted. "Dad's gonna be surprised!"

Not any more surprised than Ryanne was that she had agreed to join them. She wasn't good company, and she really didn't want to face Nick after the night before. She went to the back steps to get her tennis shoes, and followed her neighbors across the yard with dread.

Chapter Two

The back door opened. "Could have told you," Nick said.

Ryanne glanced around the remodeled kitchen. The room looked nothing like the way she remembered it. "Told me what?"

Nick's head shot around. He met her eyes with a look of total surprise.

Mel and Jamie entered the kitchen behind her.

"Your dad invited me to breakfast," she explained.

Mel had always been kind to her, had always seemed like the kind of parent a kid would want. He'd taken time to play ball with her and Nick and Justin, drive them to the community pool and drop them off at movies. She had no beef with Mel Sinclair. Mel hadn't seemed like the type of person her father had always warned her was looking to judge their family.

She liked Mel Sinclair, so she was here was for his sake.

Nick jumped out of his seat and went to the cupboard for another plate.

"Ryanne's gonna eat with us, Dad," Jamie said cheerfully. "Ain't that cool?"

"That's definitely cool." Nick nodded to the bright, sunlit breakfast nook with padded benches. "Have a seat."

"Gosh, it's good to see you," Mel said, sitting across from her and next to Jamie, leaving Nick the space beside Ryanne. Nick had picked up his plate and carried it away already. "You've been such a stranger," Mel continued. "I want to hear all about your life."

"Thank you." She accepted the glass of orange juice Nick placed in front of her. "Not much to tell, really."

"What do you mean? Your mother told us about your company and how successful you've been. That's just great."

She managed a weak smile. Just great. "Yeah."

"And your husband," the older man added. "The two of you run the company together?"

Nick held a cup and a glass coffeepot toward her, with a questioning lift of one dark brow.

"Yes, thanks. I'd love a cup."

"It's decaf," Mel said with a note of displeasure. "Nick has decaffeinated us."

"That's okay." She watched Nick's strong, steady hand pour a mugful and set it before her.

"How come you didn't take your vacation in Arizona with your mother?" Mel asked.

"Vacation?"

The old man nodded. "Seems you picked the time of year to come here when most people are heading other directions."

"Oh, well, I, um, I needed…"

All three of them gazed at her expectantly, Nick awaiting her reply from in front of the stove.

"I needed…" A place to run? Somewhere to stay that wouldn't cost her anything? "A change," she said finally.

Nick resumed dishing up her food.

"I'll bet an important job like that gets stressful," Mel said with a sympathetic cluck.

A minute later, Nick set down a plate holding a complete breakfast. She raised her gaze. "You fixed this?"

Nick nodded and sat beside her. He wore a navy-blue T-shirt that fit his muscular body like a second skin, and she couldn't help stealing an appreciative glance. He was so much…*bigger* than she remembered. Muscular arms, strong hands… How weird of her to take notice. Of course he'd developed into a man.

"Dad always makes us breakfast on Saturday," Jamie told her. "Sometimes on Sunday, too. But sometimes we go to the Waggin' Tongue and Miss Rumford makes me pancakes shaped like animals. Dad tried it, but they all looked like blobs."

Nick shrugged and picked up his mug. "We all have our talents. Shirley Rumford's is buffalo pancakes."

"Does Harry Ulrich still run the place with her?"

Ryanne asked, tasting her pancakes and finding them delicious.

Nick affirmed that he did. The couple had run the bar and grill as partners and friends for thirty years.

"Still just the one grocery store in town?" she asked.

"Turner Foods. Norm owns it now. His dad is in the nursing home."

"I'd better make a trip over there today and get a few items. I really appreciate you inviting me to breakfast. All I found were a few canned things, and none of them appealed this morning."

"You're welcome."

"Heck, you kids practically ate all your meals together at one time," Mel said. "Made it easier on your mothers, I think." His expression took on a sadness that touched Ryanne, and he gazed out the window. "I sure do miss those days. Sometimes I can still see us all in this place the way it used to be, Florence at the stove in her apron, you and Nick and Justin thundering in to wash up."

Ryanne's mother and Florence Sinclair had been best friends. Ryanne couldn't remember a summer without a family vacation together. She and Nick, with his younger brother tagging along, had been a combo ever since she could remember.

Mel had lost his wife to cancer and a year later his youngest son to a car accident. Both deaths had occurred after Ryanne had started college. She'd come back for both funerals, and she remembered the Sinclairs' grief vividly. She had shared it. "I adored Florence," she told the older man. "She was a special person."

He nodded, blinking.

Without forethought, she reached across the table and covered his hand with hers. "She used to take us to the library once a week," she told him, remembering happier days.

Mel smiled wistfully and turned his hand over to hold hers.

"There was a book I checked out over and over, so many times, in fact, that the librarian finally said I could only have it once a month, because no one else was getting to read it."

"What was the book?" Jamie asked.

"It was a story about a girl and a pet falcon. And do you know what?" she said to the boy. "Your grandma bought me a copy of that book and gave it to me so I'd have my very own."

"She did?"

Ryanne nodded. "I still have it." She'd seen it last night when she'd been rearranging things in her closet. She made a mental note to get it out and share it with Jamie.

"I don't have any grammas," Jamie told her.

Mel's hold on her hand tightened to a gentle squeeze. She met his somber eyes for a moment, then turned her attention to Jamie.

"I'm sorry," she said, and she and Mel broke the contact.

"Don't have a mom, neither," he said, his voice small and his expression serious.

Her heart hitched in her chest. She remembered then, hearing her mother mention something a long time ago about Nick's wife, but Ryanne couldn't remember what it had been. She couldn't think of anything to say.

"Dad says Miss Lottie and Miss Kris are my female role models," Jamie told her seriously.

Ryanne glanced at Nick, and he gave her a sideways smile. "His day care providers."

"It's not day care, *Dad!* I'm too big for that!"

"Right. Sorry. Summer day-camp."

Knowledge of role models seemed far too astute for a young boy. "How old are you?" Ryanne asked.

"Seven."

"Going on thirty," Nick said wryly.

"He always says that."

"Yeah, well, I'll get some new material one of these days."

"Where's your kids?" Jamie asked her.

"I don't have any."

"How come?"

"Jamie, that's none of your business," his father reprimanded.

"Well, I was wonderin', is all. Be cool if I had a kid next door to play with like you guys did when you was little."

"You have Wade," Nick reminded him.

"Yeah," Jamie agreed, and said to Ryanne, "Wade is my bestest friend. We do stuff together."

"Do you remember Forrest Perry?" Nick asked her. "Wade is one of Forrest and Natalie's kids."

"I remember," she said. "The quarterback."

Nick grinned. "That was a long time ago."

"Natalie. Wasn't she the girl who used to set up a lemonade stand on the curb and charge us a quarter a cup?'' Ryanne held up her thumb and forefinger barely two inches apart. ''A really little cup.''

Nick chuckled. ''Same one. Forrest has the car dealership on the highway now. Natalie is president of the PTA. They're Scout leaders.''

Mel and Jamie had finished their meal, and Ryanne, too, laid down her fork. ''That was great.''

''You need any help washing that car?'' Jamie asked.

''Thanks, but I think I'm done.''

''Okay. Well, ask me next time you need help, and I'll come on over.''

''Will do.''

''Me 'n' Grampa are gonna go fishin'!''

''We'd better go see if the night crawlers in the fridge in the garage are still squirmin','' Mel said.

''Want I should help you with the dishes?'' Jamie asked his dad.

''Nope. You two go on.'' Nick crouched down and Jamie gave him a bear hug. He tousled his son's hair. ''I love you, little mister.''

''I love you, big mister. See ya, Ryanne!''

She waved. ''Have fun.''

Seeing the interaction between father and son touched her unexpectedly. Nick gathered dishes to rinse and load into the dishwasher. She carried two glasses and he took them.

Feeling awkward now that were alone, she leaned back against a counter and surveyed the room. The breakfast nook bay was a new addition, as well as the center island. Appliances in an almond shade had replaced the old ones. The sink had been moved to a different wall, and louvered white folding doors closed over what was probably a laundry area. A built-in desk near the doorway to the dining room housed a computer and a phone. The bulletin board behind it was covered with notes and childish drawings—mostly of cars.

"Doesn't even look like the same room," she commented.

He straightened from the dishwasher. "I'd forgotten you'd never seen it. We did this about six years ago. We spend a lot of time in here, and the place was out of date. Dad has a couple of rooms and a bathroom down here now, too."

In contrast, her mother's house hadn't changed a bit. Even the furnishings were the same as they'd been for as long as Ryanne could recall. The difference between the two homes was like night and day.

"Care for another cup of coffee?" Nick asked.

"No thanks, I have to be going."

He nodded and turned to pick up a skillet.

"I'm sorry about last night," she told him, forcing the words out before she lost her nerve.

He paused, touching the handle of the pan. "Me, too."

"No, really. You were looking out for the place and I was being a jerk."

"I embarrassed you. I'm sorry about that."

She picked up a damp dish towel and folded it into a square. "Think we can forget about that?"

He turned his head and looked her in the eye.

She'd looked into those eyes a thousand times, whether sharing a joke, planning mischief or seeing empathy as he listened to her share a problem. But this was different. She recognized the same change she'd noticed last night, the difference that had made her uncomfortable then. He shouldn't have been looking at her that way.

His gaze slid to the front of her shirt in a completely assessing and direct manner. Her cheeks grew uncomfortably warm. Even though his air-conditioned home was at least ten degrees cooler than the air outside, her whole body seemed too warm. His perusal traveled downward over her shorts and the length of her legs, then back up to her face. "Probably not."

That was wrong. He'd seen her in her underwear before. Her mother had a home movie of them playing in a wading pool in their underpants, for heaven's sake! Even though Ryanne was two years older than Nick, she'd considered him a friend and a confidant all through high school.

Never in all those times had their relationship waded into these unfamiliar waters. She didn't think she liked the turn it had taken. "Probably not? What does that mean?"

He turned back to his task. "You figure it out."

"What kind of cop-out comment is that?"

"Let it go, Rye," he said.

His words angered her, but at the same time the vulnerability in them touched her. She forced her mind to release the questions she'd formed. She'd come over here for Mel's sake, not for a heart-to-heart or to make amends with Nick, and it was past time to leave. His apology had been unexpected.

But strangely welcome, she admitted to herself.

She hung the towel on a hook. Her head was too messed up to get into anything like this, and all she wanted was to be left to herself, anyway. "Thanks again."

"Anytime."

"Bye." She was out the door before he could reply. All the way across the yard that separated their houses, she felt like she was being watched. Maybe he was standing at the back door, watching her go. Maybe the neighbors were on full alert, garnering news for the rumor mill. She glanced at the houses that had been built across the alley behind their yards in the last ten or so years.

When she reached her driveway, she looked toward the west at the house on the other side, and saw Audrey Milligan in blue polyester pants and Reebok running shoes, watering her rose bushes. At least some things never changed. The blue-haired woman waved. "Hi, sweetie! I didn't know you were home!"

Picking up her bucket and supplies and carrying them to the garage, Ryanne replied, "Yes, just taking a little vacation."

"We're having ice cream in the park tomorrow night. Don't forget to join us."

Ryanne waved and smiled and put away her bucket. Her Viper was dry, so she pulled it into the garage to protect the paint from the sun.

She put it in Park, checked the windows and ran her palms over the luxurious leather seat beneath her bottom. A bundle of mail she'd picked up before leaving had fallen to the floor and been buried under bags and boxes, so she picked it up now, closed and locked the wooden garage doors, and carried the mail to the house.

She reached for the knob on the back door, realizing she hadn't locked it before leaving. Nobody ever locked their doors in Elmwood; she'd forgotten that. In fact, anyone locking a door usually got yelled at, because people didn't carry keys. The interior door stuck for a moment, but swung inward after she gave it a healthy shove.

Ryanne tossed the envelopes on the table and glanced around the kitchen. The refrigerator was one of those old ones with rounded corners and big coils on the back. The faucets on the sink were the old-fashioned enamel kind, and the cast-iron sink itself had a fabric skirt around the bottom. Clean and tidy. In good repair.

She pulled out a chrome and red vinyl chair and sat. Three of the envelopes were from the IRS. The others were assorted bills. The jerk had even charged airfare and clothing on a credit card before he left.

One letter was from a former client, expressing his condolences over her situation. How many of them had learned the truth through the grapevine? She had told a few in person, but the whole process had been too humiliating, and she'd forsaken the rest of her list.

Ryanne buried her head in her hands. The wonder girl of Griffin Park had been laid low. By now everyone knew. She thought back over the past two years and tried again to understand how she'd never suspected Mason. She was a fool, and anyone as foolish as she'd been deserved to be taken. She'd thought and considered and wondered until she'd driven herself crazy with self-condemnation.

But even understanding how it had happened, or knowing exactly when and what her ex-husband had done to undermine her and their company, wouldn't fix the problem. Nothing but a wad of cash was going to pacify the government. And she was fresh out of cash.

She lowered her face, and the laminate tabletop felt cool against her cheek. She was a person of action. She shouldn't be sitting here feeling sorry for herself. She couldn't wait for the anger to leave, or for the humiliation and shock to wear off. She could be waiting until people in hell got that ice water.

She had a prescription, something to take the edge off when the hellish thoughts got really bad, but she hated taking the pills. She'd taken them for a week before she realized that not feeling at all was worse than being miserable, and she'd stopped.

Taking action, she got up and went into the dining room, where she'd stacked boxes containing her stereo equipment and computer. She would put the stereo together first. That way she could listen to her CDs, play something soothing.

Then she'd get hook up the computer and get online. She had a résumé to update and research to do. She was going to fix her life. Or die crying.

Later that afternoon Nick hoed along a row of pole beans and bent to pull weeds away from his watermelon plants. The beating sun was hot on his back and shoulders, and sweat ran down his spine, but the humidity hadn't kicked in yet. He straightened and stretched. The sun and heat lent a torpid tiredness that felt sinfully good. It would be great to lie down and sleep. Close his eyes and let blankness close around him, block out everything.

He pulled off his cap, closed his eyes and raised

his face to the sun. Bright light was supposed to shut off melatonin production, but when he got out here he sure felt like he could sleep.

But he couldn't do it. Daytime sleeping was on his list of no-nos, no matter how tempting it was, no matter how tired he got, no matter how much exhaustion overcame him. No, in fact—he pulled on his cap and glanced at his watch—this was his scheduled time for worrying.

He scoffed at himself, but had to believe this strategy was working. Since grief and regret and worry were the things that kept him from sleeping nights, he was supposed to get them out of the way during the day. Thing was, he didn't *want* to think about this stuff. He wanted to put it behind him and forget about it. Dragging it out and dwelling on it deliberately seemed warped.

But he thought anyway—morbid speculation coming to him unbidden at night, stealing sleep, stealing peace—so the theory was to get it over with during the day.

All right. *Justin.* Today his dad had seemed melancholy when he'd spoken to Ryanne about the past. Every time Justin's name came from his father's mouth, Nick felt responsible for his pain. For years, all Nick had been able to do was think of all the ways he could have prevented Justin's death. Hindsight was indeed twenty-twenty, as the old saying went.

He'd been nineteen years old, trying to work and go to college, taking responsibility for a rebellious kid brother with no mother and a father who had to work two jobs to support them. Justin had been in so many scrapes that Nick had ceased telling their father about them, sparing him the added worry. Nick's mother had barely been gone a year, and Mel was still grieving.

Only the week before Justin's death, Nick had received a call from him, asking Nick to come get him in a nearby town. He'd been with friends at a party where there had been drinking. When deputies were called to the scene, Justin had managed to run away and call home.

The night of Justin's death, Nick had been in the garage, finally taking a couple of hours to work on the Chevy he'd been restoring, and Justin had stopped in, asking Nick to accompany him to a party.

"Come on, Nick, loosen up and have a little fun. Come with us," he'd said.

"You'd better not be drinking again this time."

"I'm not hurting anybody. Geez, you're so uptight, you'd think I was killing somebody."

Nick had looked him over impatiently. "All you ever think about is fun. You never think ahead to what it's going to cost. I'm tired of coming to your rescue, Justin. I'm tired of covering for you. Stop. Look at what you're doing and grow up."

"I'm still a kid," he'd argued. "I have plenty of time to grow up, not that I want to. I don't want to be a downer like you. Come with us. You can keep me out of trouble."

"I shouldn't have to watch over your every move. Use your head, for cryin' out loud."

"I just want to have some fun."

"Getting hammered and driving is not fun," Nick argued.

"You're so lame," Justin complained. "You'd think you were my father, instead of my brother."

Nick had seen red at that. He liked to have as much fun as the next person, he just had more on his mind and less free time. In frustration, he threw a wrench across the garage, where it hit the wall and clanged to the cement floor with a harmless clatter. "Why can't you see? Someone has to take some responsibility! Life isn't all fun and games. Those friends of yours are losers."

"You're just jealous because I have friends to hang out with!" Justin kicked a metal trash can and headed away from the garage. "What about Holly? Is she a loser, too?"

"My guess is you're disappointing her too."

"You don't know anything about me and Holly."

"Stay out of trouble, Justin. I'm not coming to bail you out this time."

"I never asked you to."

"Oh? Who was that who called me last Friday night to come get him at 2:00 a.m.? Sure sounded like you. Looked like you when I got there, too."

Justin yanked open his car door. "Go to hell, Nick. I don't need you."

"Good. Because I have a life, too."

"Yeah, I can see that. You and your honey, there. Have a real good time together tonight."

With hurt and anger making his head ache, Nick had watched the taillights of Justin's car disappear down the lane.

He had worked on the carburetor until he was so tired his eyes burned and his vision blurred, then he'd scrubbed his hands and nails, showered and sat at the kitchen table with a can of soda and a sandwich. He'd been turning off the lights to go to bed when the phone rang.

Mentally gathering himself for another plea for help, and fully expecting bad news, he hadn't been a bit surprised when the voice at the other end of the line had been Sheriff Cody's.

"I need to talk to your father, Son," the man had said gently.

"He's asleep, Sheriff. He has to get up early. I can handle the problem."

"Not this time, Nick. I really need you to go wake up your dad."

"What is it?" he asked, his anger turning to fear. "Has something happened?"

"Get your dad, Son."

With a sick feeling in his stomach, Nick had placed the receiver on the counter and sprinted up the stairs to his father's room. Roused from sleep, Mel had slouched on the side of the bed and reached for the phone on the bedside table. "This is Mel Sinclair. What? When? How bad? Oh my God. Oh my God."

Nick's heart had raced painfully, waiting for the bad news that was to come. He'd never forgotten the words, the stricken look on his father's face, the gut-wrenching feeling of shame and guilt. Nick heard the words every night when he tried to sleep, saw his father's face, felt his anguish all the way to his soul.

He could have been there. He could have gone along. He could have prevented Justin from driving his car. He could have spared his father from losing a son.

The perfectly tuned throb of a powerful engine, the

sound like a Beethoven concerto to a music lover's ears, brought Nick out of his depressing musings. He glanced toward the house next door and saw the red Viper glide into the driveway and pull to a smooth stop at the rear of the house. The engine cut. The door on the far side opened and Ryanne got out. She was still wearing those shorts. *Damn.*

With a purse slung over her shoulder, and clutching several bulging plastic grocery bags, she glanced his way.

She'd caught him looking, so he gave a hesitant wave. Hands full, she nodded and smiled.

He went back to his weeds, trying not to notice the way her shorts hugged her backside and left her slender thighs exposed as she climbed the stairs. The scorching image of her in her miniscule underwear had been burned into his retinas. Could he forget it? Ha. Not in this lifetime.

The jingle of her keys reached him. The plastic bags rustled. Nick glanced up to see her holding the screen open while jiggling the lock and leaning against the heavy door. She set her purse down on the small wooden platform that served as a back porch, used the leather bag to prop the screen door open, and tried again.

After a couple of minutes, Nick removed his work gloves, wiped his palms against his faded jeans and walked over. ''Can I give you a hand?''

She glanced up, her hair tucked behind an ear, exasperation plain on her flustered face. ''I don't know what's the matter with the darned thing. It stuck this morning, too, but I got it open by pushing.''

Nick climbed the stairs. Her gaze flitted uncomfortably across his bare chest. He hadn't had a shirt handy to pull on. To give her somewhere else to look, he pushed his sunglasses up on his head. She met his eyes, hesitation and embarrassment obvious in the blue depths of hers. "I didn't think anybody locked their doors around here," he said.

She shrugged. "Old habits are hard to break."

Was it just that they'd once been close friends and that her expressions were all sweetly familiar that he thought her so lovely? He didn't believe so. She had the widest blue eyes he'd ever seen, and her lips were full and soft-looking. Half a dozen shots and a concussion wouldn't dull the ardor that was giving him an ache in his groin. "Let me try it once."

"What?" Her cheeks turned pink. "Oh." She dangled the set of keys toward him, the door key pinched between her fingers and thumb.

Nick took them, their hands brushing.

She stepped back like a stranger would. They were strangers now, after all. And she was a married woman.

He inserted the key and it turned in the lock immediately. The door itself, however, wouldn't budge. He inspected the wood. "No dead bolt inside or anything?"

"Nope."

"Must be swollen from the heat." He leaned a shoulder against it and shoved.

With a wrenching sound, the door popped open.

Nick stepped into the doorway and examined the frame. "I can plane a little off here and here, and it'll work fine."

"I don't want you to go to any trouble," she said uneasily, a frown creasing her forehead.

He looked at her over his shoulder. She'd picked up her purse and the groceries. "It'll take five minutes. Your mom always lets me fix things for her."

Ryanne raised one brow. "I could do it myself if you want to loan me the plane."

"What are neighbors for?"

She seemed reluctant, but finally nodded in acquiescence.

Nick stepped past her, out onto the stoop. "I'll be right back."

Before he went to the garage for his tools, he entered his kitchen for the T-shirt he'd left on the back of a chair, and pulled it on, hanging his sunglasses from the neck opening.

When he returned, the door stood open, and Ryanne was nowhere in sight. He took the opportunity to walk around the gleaming red car, peek through the window at the dash and check out the speedometer. He'd heard these things could really move.

"I got it up to 178 on a straightaway coming through Nevada," she said from the back door.

Damn. Busted, drooling on her fender.

Chapter Three

He turned away from the car, but didn't meet her eyes. "Seriously," he said.

"Seriously."

"Have any idea how dangerous that was?"

"You mean because of the cops, Sheriff?"

"Risky with your life, I mean."

"Yeah, well, you only live once. Might as well go out in style."

Her flippant remark hit him like a gut punch, but he masked it quickly. That daredevil attitude had always driven him crazy, and she knew it. But she hadn't meant it, not really. She wasn't careless. She'd made something of her life, hadn't wasted herself like Justin had. Nick raised his gaze to look at her through the screen.

She shrugged, a gesture that seemed more offhand

than he believed she truly was. She turned and disappeared back inside.

He took a hammer and a screwdriver and loosened the bolts that held the wooden door, then removed them and maneuvered the door from its hinges and down the back stairs. He laid it on the ground, then propped it on edge between his knees, and planed aged paint and a thin layer of wood from the offending spots.

Inside the kitchen, silverware tinkled and water ran.

Finished, he smoothed sandpaper over the edges, then climbed the stairs and used the sandpaper on the door frame, too.

"Still like lemonade?" she asked from inside.

He glanced into the kitchen, the interior dim after the bright sunlight. Nothing in the room ever changed. A chrome table and chairs stood beneath the window. The refrigerator was one of those squatty antiquities with rounded corners. "I still like it. You gonna charge me a quarter?"

She opened the refrigerator and the small metal door of the freezer, then jimmied out an ice cube tray, a motion that made her butt wiggle. "Heard of inflation here in Iowa?" she called. "Lemonade is a buck fifty now."

Nick chuckled, finished the sanding and carried the door back. "I'm going to need you to help me line up the hinges."

She stood behind the door and helped him guide it into place.

Leaning back slightly, he fished in his hip pocket, then held the bolts out to her. "Can you slip them in if I hold it steady?"

She had to take his hammer and tap the hinges gently to get them aligned, and within a few minutes they were finished. The door opened and shut smoothly.

"Perfect," she said.

"It's a good solid door."

She rinsed her hands and poured lemonade into a red aluminum glass that chilled his fingers.

He studied the tumbler. "I haven't seen one of these in years."

"Remember those little terry-cloth things Mom used to slip on them to keep them from sweating? I could probably find them in a drawer, if I looked."

He grinned. "Yeah."

Her discomfort with his presence seemed to have lessened, but she was probably just feeling indebted because of the door. Their years as childhood friends seemed like another lifetime.

The tart lemonade was sweet and ice-cold, and tasted like summer. Nick drank it all and she poured him a second glass.

"You always could drink an ocean of lemonade," she said.

He met her eyes, and her expression grew shuttered, as though she regretted the words that had alluded to how well they'd once known each other.

The urge to ask if she was all right crowded into his mind. Her skittish reluctance to hold his gaze was uncharacteristic of the girl he remembered, as was her seeming uncertainty and the nervous way she swept the hair away from her neck. But it had been a long time since he'd said more than a passing hello to her. How would he know what she was like now? He couldn't help wondering what was she doing here and where her husband was.

Nick held his questions in check. She didn't owe him any explanations. And he should respect her privacy.

He finished off his second glass. "I have a couple of rows left to weed," he said finally, pushing away from the counter where he'd leaned.

"Your garden looks nice. You do it all yourself?"

He nodded. "Dad can't take the sun anymore. He waters in the morning or the evening if it's cool enough."

"You have a lot of beans there. Don't tell me you can them, too, besides cooking a mean breakfast."

He set the glass he'd used in the sink. "Hardly. I freeze 'em."

"Thanks for your help."

"No problem."

Outside, he bent to pick up his toolbox from the wooden platform, and Ryanne noted the muscles in his long thighs beneath his jeans as he moved. Thank goodness he'd pulled on a T-shirt, though it did little to disguise the broad planes of his chest and back as he worked. The fact that *this* was Nick Sinclair still had her flabbergasted. Who'd have imagined it? Every time he drew close, his surprising size gave her a hitch in her chest.

Nick Sinclair was supposed to remain the boy of her memories, but everything about him screamed *man*. Those muscled arms, that wide chest. Over six foot of solid man, a man who looked as good in his jeans and T-shirt as he had in the uniform.

He said goodbye, and she waved him off, catching

herself admiring his backside as he carried the tool-box to his garage.

She latched the flimsy hook on the screen door, rinsed the two glasses and the spoon she'd used, and placed the pitcher of lemonade in the refrigerator, standing with the door open for a moment to cool her flushed skin.

She couldn't remember the last time she'd said more than a few polite words to Nick at a wedding or funeral. It had been years and years since they'd been close. So he really should feel more like a stranger to her than he did.

The difference in his appearance should have been enough to scare her off completely. The last thing she needed was any kind of entanglement with a male.

The older they'd grown, the less she'd had in common with this particular one, anyway. Tinkering with cars and growing vegetables still seemed to be his passion, and he'd never understood the driving need she'd had to prove herself.

Immediately, she swallowed tears. And what good had it all done? Ryanne closed the refrigerator door and turned to wipe the counter. At least Nick seemed content, and he had a son who adored him. She certainly had nothing to show for all her years away from here. Nothing except a broken spirit and a staggering debt.

The image of her husband loomed up before her, and she squeezed out the dishcloth with frightening intensity. The familiar sick feeling that always swept over her when she thought of Mason curled around her now, and she pinched her eyes shut, the lemonade in her stomach turning sour.

Don't give in to the panic. Don't give in to it, she told herself fiercely, forcing her posture straight and her eyes open. *He isn't worth it. You're better off without him.*

No one knew. That was her single, tiny consolation.

Hanging the dishcloth and towel, she made her way to the dining room, where she'd set up her computer. In the worst heat of the day, this was the only room that stayed bearable, with the help of the ancient window fan drawing the humid air out, and the shade of the three oak trees in the side yard. She didn't dare run the air-conditioning and add to the electric bill.

Unpacking a box of software and data disks, she came across the accounting files Mason had kept for the agency. His handwriting on the label jumped out at her. She started to throw the disk toward the wall, needing to vent a mere tenth of a degree of the anger and hurt that dwelled inside her, but she paused and calmed herself. There might be something on it she'd need later.

Tossing it on the lace-covered dining table, she clenched her fists ineffectually, dropping her head back to gaze at the ceiling.

For as long as she could remember, she'd observed her mother's subservience to her husband, a college professor with special "needs" and "position" in the community. Ryanne had determined she would be satisfied with nothing less than being a success on her own. She'd damn near made it, too. She'd earned the degrees, launched the business, worked her tail off....

And her ex was living high on the hog in some

country with no extradition. Spending her money. Probably spending it on a woman. Or two.

The betrayal hurt like hell. She'd never been so angry with anyone in her life. Never been so humiliated. But the fact that the other women didn't *hurt* had been a revelation. Ryanne had realized somewhere during the last couple of years that she'd never really loved Mason.

She'd been impressed with his abilities, taken with his drive and ambition, which she'd believed matched hers, and thought that they'd make a dynamite team. And they had. In business only. And while it lasted.

The phone rang. No one except her mother and the neighbors had this number, so Ryanne didn't have to worry about dodging bill collectors. "Hello?"

"Hi, honey."

"Mom. I didn't expect you to call."

"I was just wondering how you're doing."

"I'm doing fine."

"Are you sure everything's okay, Ryanne? You've never done anything like this before. Do you need me there?"

"Oh, no, Mom. That's not necessary. I just came for a vacation, is all."

"A vacation? In Elmwood? Something's not right, and I know it. Are you and Mason having problems?"

Ryanne listened to the genuine concern in her mother's voice and a crack opened in her steely resolve. She hadn't been able to tell anyone, hadn't had anyone with whom to share this dismal episode in her life. She'd felt as though saying the words would be admitting her failure, and she hadn't been ready to do that. But she was tired of the solitary struggle...and of avoiding the truth. She released a breath and felt the prickle of hot tears. "Yes, Mom. Mason and I have had a lot of problems. We're not living together anymore."

"Oh," her mother said, her voice breaking. "I'm so sorry, honey. I'm sure you'll be able to work things out if you both give it some time and—"

"I divorced him, Mom. Quite a while ago. I—I just didn't have the courage to tell you. I'm sorry."

"Oh, honey." Her mother was silent for a long moment. "I had a feeling it was something like that," she said finally. "I'm so sorry. And I'm sorry you didn't feel you could share it with me."

"No. It's not you, Mom. It's me. It's always been me."

"I'll come right away if you want."

"No. I just need some time. I'm starting my life over, and it's going to take some getting used to. I know you understand that. I mean, after Daddy leaving and all."

"I do. That's why I like it here so much, I guess. Nothing to remind me of him and the way it used to be. Do you hear from your dad?"

"A card at Christmas. He phoned on my birthday. He and his new wife Brittney took a trip to Japan in the spring. I didn't even get a postcard."

"I'm sorry, dear. I know how his leaving hurt you."

"Me? I think you're the one with the bone to pick, Mom."

Her mother chuckled. "You know, I think he did me a favor. I wouldn't have been able to say that until the last few years, but I'm really enjoying my life here.''

''Good for you.''

''You can come visit if you like.''

Ryanne considered it, then remembered the cost of plane fare, and said evasively, ''I'll think about it.''

''All right. Call me anytime. Is everything all right at the house? I would have called Nick and had him turn on the air-conditioning for you, but I didn't know when you'd arrive.''

''It's not that hot here,'' she lied. ''But I want you to let me know if there are extra costs from me staying at the house. You get the statements there, right?''

''Yes, but I'm sure it won't be much.''

''Nick fixed the back door for me this afternoon. It stuck and I couldn't get it open.''

''He's such a sweetheart, that young man,'' Evelyn said. ''Isn't it a shame he doesn't have a wife who deserves him?''

''Where is his wife?'' Ryanne asked, now that she had the opportunity. Once she'd left, she hadn't really paid any attention to the people back in Elmwood.

''Don't you remember? Holly left him when little Jamie was barely two. She was never happy. Maybe she never got over Justin. I never really thought she was Nick's type. Mel told me the two of them had a lot of problems and she finally just signed over custody and took off.''

''How sad for Jamie.''

''Yes, he's a great little boy.''

''Holly was Justin's girlfriend, right?''

''Yes. But after Justin's death—not long actually, maybe not even quite a year—she and Nick got married. There was a lot of speculation over that relationship, as you can guess.''

"There's always been a lot of speculation over everything in this town. And Mom?''

"What?''

"I haven't told anyone about me and Mason. So if you talk to anyone, please don't say anything.''

"I won't, dear. I rarely talk with folks in Elmwood unless I'm there for a stay.''

"Thank you.''

"And call me if you need me,'' her mother added. "Call Nick if you need something quickly.''

"I'll be just fine.''

"You're always just fine, but sometimes we need other people. You've always thought you had to be so independent that you couldn't even ask for help.''

"Okay. If I need help, I'll ask.''

"Good. I love you. Bye, honey.''

"Bye, Mom. I love you.'' Ryanne hung up the phone, relieved to have told someone, yet saddened by the reality.

Children's laughter reached her.

She walked to the window where the enormous old fan rattled, sucking out air, but barely making a difference. Through the window above the fan, she observed a ball game in progress. Nick, clad in jeans but shirtless, wearing a ball cap backward, was playing ball with half a dozen boys wearing caps in the same fashion. Wasn't the whole point of a brim to keep the sun out of one's eyes? She smiled to herself.

Watching Nick encouraging the kids and chasing the ball, throwing it and smacking the palm of his leather glove, she had to agree with her mother. It was a shame Nick didn't have a wife who deserved him. Well, it was a shame Jamie didn't have a mother—Ryanne couldn't really say what kind of a wife Nick deserved. It was none of her business, anyway.

And the last thing she should be thinking about.

Ryanne had worked well into the night, updating and polishing her résumé until she had a package she believed was impressive. Now, where to send it? She spent Sunday morning washing curtains and bedding and checking out career opportunities on the Web. When the church bell rang from a few streets away, dozens of nostalgic memories interrupted her thinking.

She carried a cup of coffee to the front door and studied the deserted street and neighborhood. Everyone had gone to one of the services at the two well-preserved church buildings the town founders had built a hundred years ago.

She glanced at the Sinclair home and the flourishing green garden. A spattering noise during the night had drawn her out here in her nightshirt to discover Nick watering his garden in the darkness. Later, she'd seen his light on. Well, if that was still his bedroom, it had been his light. It had to be, if Mel slept downstairs. Surely Jamie wasn't up until the wee hours of the morning.

She finished her research, printing out a few pages she wanted to review, and carried them out to the open porch.

Mistake.

Neighbors were making their way home from

church, walking along the tree-shaded street. She recognized Russel Carter and his wife, Janet, who lived
a few houses away. Russel owned and ran the Second
Chance Used Furniture Store. The couple spotted her
and waved vigorously.

Ryanne returned the greeting, and they turned up
her walk. "Ryanne Whitaker," Russel said with a
wide smile. "It's sure been a long time since we've
seen you around here."

"Yeah, I guess it has. How are you?"

"We're just fine, thanks, and you?"

"Great, great. You still selling furniture?"

"Buying and selling," he said with a nod.

Ryanne glanced at Janet.

"I work part-time for Sheigh Addison. She's the
vet," Janet told her.

"Is she new in town? I don't remember the name."

"She's been here about five years, I guess," Janet
said, looking to her husband for confirmation.

He nodded.

"Well," Ryanne said. "Elmwood must be growing."

"Oh, it is, it is," Russel agreed. "We have a pet
store, too. Paige Duncan runs it. Does dog grooming,
too. We take our Luvey there."

"Do you have a dog?" Janet asked.

Ryanne shook her head. Janet's expression fell.
She'd obviously lost esteem in the woman's eyes.

"Well, if you get a dog, Sheigh is the best vet
you'll find."

"Thanks. I'll remember that."

They exchanged goodbyes and the Carters headed
toward home, but before Ryanne could pick up her

papers and duck into the house, another voice called out to her. Eventually, everyone who lived on her street and had walked to church called a greeting or stopped to talk.

The Sinclairs were among the last stragglers, and Ryanne figured it was because of how many people they must have stopped to talk to before they got here.

"Morning, Ryanne," Mel called.

Jamie ran up her steps and showed her the picture he'd colored, from a lesson book—showing Daniel in the lion's den.

"I like the way you use color," she told him, kneeling beside him and pointing to his work. "This is bright and eye-catching."

"Spoken as someone in advertising?" Nick asked, coming up behind his son with a smile.

She shrugged. "Maybe." She returned her attention to Jamie's drawing. "Is this going up on the bulletin board with all your other pictures?"

The child nodded. "Did you see 'em?"

"I did. You're quite an artist."

He nodded again.

"Why don't you come have lunch with us?" Mel offered from the bottom of the steps.

"Oh, thanks, but I have work to do," she replied.

"I spent a lot of years working on Sundays and I can tell you, life slips by that way," he said with a seriousness she recognized.

She glanced from him to Nick, not knowing what to say.

"But you'll be done by tonight, right?" Mel asked.

Ryanne was afraid to say one way or the other. Finally, she gave a half nod.

"Good, then we'll come by and pick you up for ice cream in the park. Nick has to take a freezer, so we'll be leaving a little early. See you around six-thirty."

Ryanne stared at Mel's back as he made his way toward home. She turned and met Nick's amused expression. "What's so funny?"

"You. Him." He chuckled.

"I don't have a burning desire to be eaten alive by mosquitoes, thank you."

"They're not even out yet. And when they are, the park gets sprayed."

"Whatever."

"We'll see you later." He took Jamie's hand and they walked away from her.

Jamie tugged on Nick's hand and Nick leaned over to listen to something he had to say. He nodded and Jamie ran back and clambered up the stairs to Ryanne. He extended the picture he'd colored. "This is for you."

Ryanne accepted it with a twinge in the area of her heart. She looked into the boy's dark blue eyes, eyes so like his father's, yet so filled with a hope and enthusiasm she no longer saw in Nick's. "Are you sure you want me to have it?"

Jamie nodded. "You don't have any pictures in your kitchen, do you?"

"No."

"You can put it on your fridgerator. And when you see it, you can remember to not be afraid. That's what the lesson was about."

Ryanne accepted the gift and thanked him. "I'll remember that."

She watched them go home and enter their house, then she gathered her papers and went inside. She finally found a butterfly magnet made out of pipe cleaners and sequins, and stuck her picture up.

Mel's words had recalled her earlier thoughts. This had been one of the few Sunday mornings for as long as she could remember that she hadn't worked. Well, she'd been working, but a Sunday that she hadn't gone into the office. It gave her a lost feeling, a feeling of not belonging and not having anything important to do.

Even though her mother held a liberal arts degree, Evelyn had always stayed home, always catered to her husband's career and needs. The waste of education and talent had always bothered Ryanne, so she'd worked hard to not fall into the same trap. She'd had an important job and a fulfilling career until now. This current lack of identity was taking a toll on her already ragged self-esteem.

The sooner she found something and got her life back, the better. She washed windows for the next hour or so, and when the curtains were dry, she carried them in off the clothesline and hung them. They smelled fresh from the sun, and she stood in the lacy pattern of shadows they created and studied the house next door.

Movement caught her eye, and she observed Nick entering the enormous detached garage. Ryanne forced herself away from the window and switched on her CD player. Maybe she'd cool off if she took a brisk shower.

A long time later, she sat in the dimness of the dining room, which was protected from the afternoon sun, and listened to the news on the radio station she'd tuned in. Seemed she'd been out of things forever.

She'd been anticipating the knock at the door, but her heart tripped anyway. She'd hoped they might forget, but of course they hadn't. Two Sinclair males stood on her porch: Nick and Jamie. "Ready?" Nick asked.

He wore a pair of tan shorts, a striped summer shirt and heavy leather sandals. Ryanne glanced at his tanned legs and feet, then drew her gaze forcefully to his face. Sunglasses and that backward ball cap completed the sexy look. The fact that she thought he was sexy was way off base.

"Do I need to bring anything?" she asked through the screen.

"Don't need anything but yourself," he replied.

She pulled the door closed behind her and followed them down the wooden steps.

Jamie fell into step beside her, Nick behind, making her self-conscious. A shiny '57 Chevy convertible, the bright aqua color of a blueberry Popsicle, waited at the curb. Mel grinned from the back seat, where he sat comfortably on the white leather seat.

Ryanne paused and looked the car over.

"This is the same kind of car you used to work on in high school," she said, somewhat awed by the perfection of the beautifully restored vehicle.

"It is," Nick replied, and opened the door for her. Jamie hopped into the back beside his grandfather.

"It is the same kind?" she asked.

"It's the same car."

"No." Her breath whooshed out. She got in and

touched the vintage dash, the chrome door handles. "It's absolutely beautiful, Nick."

"Thanks. It's my favorite," he replied easily. "Can't see getting rid of her." He slid behind the steering wheel and started the engine, driving the car away from the curb.

"No, of course not," she replied. "Your persistence obviously paid off. You must have envisioned it like this all along, while I only saw an old car."

He turned and met her eyes, and she flushed beneath his look. She hadn't meant to gush, but the car was truly a classic beauty. It had to be worth a pretty penny.

He returned his attention to the streets and in minutes they arrived at the park in the center of town. A cement fountain splashed water as it had for a century, and even the streetlights that lined all four sides were the originals, converted from gas years ago.

Two enormous, striped canvas tents had been erected, and tables and chairs carried from the courthouse across the street.

Ryanne immediately felt herself the center of attention. Someone new stood out like a third eye in this community, and she was certain that speculation about her visit had already been flying. Because of her father's warnings, she'd always felt the judgmental eye of this community on her anyway, only now it was worse.

Nick got an ice-cream freezer from his trunk and carried it to a shaded picnic table, where the ingredients and the other freezers were set out.

"There's my friend, Wade," Jamie said, pointing to the approaching family.

"What a surprise," Natalie Perry said with a smile. "I heard you were in town." She held a dark-haired little girl on her hip.

"Yes." Ryanne greeted them and admired the chubby-cheeked toddler.

"This is Wendy," Natalie told her. "That's Wade."

"They're darling children," Ryanne said sincerely.

Forrest took a business card from his wallet and handed it to her. "Come see me if you need a deal on a car."

Ryanne glanced down, noting the name Heartland Auto Deals and the address on the highway. "Okay. Thanks."

Natalie laughed. "He never gets to do that, because he already knows everyone, so just ignore him."

A young woman with strawberry-blond curls caught up in a clip on her head moved into their circle. "Ryanne! You look wonderful! Look at you!"

Recognizing her former high school friend, Ryanne couldn't get over the changes. Birdy Nichols was no longer a skinny girl with freckles and glasses, but a petite, curvy knockout.

Natalie and Forrest moved away, and Jamie followed with his little friend.

"I hardly recognized you," Ryanne told Birdy. "You look so—different!"

"Better, I hope. You, too. What size are those shorts? A five? And the highlights in your hair—great touch. I could really hate you. I work out three times a week and still look like a sausage in a pair of shorts."

Ryanne laughed. Birdy had been the only female

friend Ryanne had been close to in her younger years. She'd forgotten how good it felt to have someone talk to her so frankly.

Birdy stepped forward and hugged her in a warm, spontaneous embrace that gave Ryanne a lump in her throat.

"You do not look like a sausage. You look great." She wracked her brain to remember anything about Birdy's life. She'd received a wedding invitation years ago, but the date had conflicted with something. Her mother had mentioned Birdy a few times.

They pulled apart and Ryanne glanced around, feeling bad about not keeping in touch. "Is your husband here?"

"God, I hope not. He's not my husband anymore, and he's been gone for three years. If I had to see him, I'd move away myself."

As Birdy was speaking, Nick came over to stand beside them.

Ryanne glanced at him, then at her old friend. "Oh." She felt terrible for bringing it up. "I'm sorry."

"Yeah, me too, but what the hell? Hey, Nick."

"Birdy."

"How about you?" the young woman said, directing her attention back to Ryanne. "Your marriage still intact?"

Heat washed up Ryanne's cheeks. She met Nick's interested gaze, and looked away quickly, her stomach clenching. How on earth was she going to reply to that?

Chapter Four

Ryanne considered all the lies she could tell. No one would ever know. She'd never brought Mason to Elmwood with her; even her mother had met him only a few times. No one would be the wiser if she let them think she was happily married and successful at her career.

But Birdy's flippant candor had had an effect on her. Ryanne could tell the truth, like her old friend. *She* had divorced *him,* after all. "Not exactly," she replied.

"Not exactly? How not exactly?" Birdy asked. She knelt briefly to adjust the strap on one of her hot-pink sandals with three-inch-thick soles.

Nick was gazing off toward the group of small boys playing kick ball, as if hc wasn't paying attention, but she knew he was listening.

"We're divorced." Heat fused Ryanne's cheeks with the painful admission.

"Happens to the best of us, eh, Nick?" Birdy asked with a shrug, and stood back up.

"Yeah." Nick turned to study Ryanne with an intensity she wanted to run from, but instead she looked him in the eyes and raised her chin a notch.

"At least neither of us had any kids," Birdy continued. "Not that I don't think your kid is great, Nick, because he is, but I couldn't have coped with the whole single parent thing."

"You do what you have to do," he replied.

"You don't have any kids, do you, Ryanne?" she asked.

Ryanne shook her head and glanced away. "No."

A commotion rose from the direction of the bandstand.

"Oh geez, I'm going to have to show them again how to connect the loudspeakers to the portable stereo. Catch ya in a few."

Nick watched Birdy hurriedly wobbling toward the gazebo, then turned guarded blue eyes on Ryanne. "Birdy never changes."

She didn't know what to say. Nick had been in this town all along, participating in local activities and staying current with the populace. She was just discovering what had happened since she'd left. Neither of them added anything to the discussion on their single statuses, and Nick didn't ask any questions, for which she was grateful.

Ryanne glanced around, suddenly feeling more out of place than ever.

"Want to help make ice cream?" he asked finally.

"I've never done it."

"You can be my assistant and turn the crank."

"Okay." Appearing busy and staying with Nick would keep her from falling prey to curious neighbors.

The machines were electric, so there was nothing to the process, except adding ingredients and timing the freezers. Nick had been kidding about the cranking. Once each batch of ice cream was stirred up, they scraped the cold confection into buckets set in coolers of ice.

The high school band warmed up, then played several selections from the lacy shade of the gazebo. Children ran and dogs barked, and Ryanne was transported back to her childhood. She could picture herself with Nick, Justin tagging along, as the three unconcernedly played and ate ice cream.

Since her father had forbidden his wife to mingle with Elmwood citizens not involved in the college, Mel and Florence Sinclair had packed Ryanne along to local functions. Ryanne's father believed it was beneath his position as a professor to attend such activities. Occasionally, if he'd been away or busy at the college, Evelyn Whitaker had come along, too.

Influenced by his teaching and authority, Ryanne had begun to draw away like her father when she'd reached her teens.

With the task of ice cream making finished, Nick scooped up two enormous cones and handed her one. "Let's go listen to the band. They're pretty good this year."

"I'll never eat all this."

"I'll finish what you can't." Instead of leading her

toward one of the tables, he found a shade tree and sat on the ground at its base. Ryanne settled in beside him.

They ate their rich, smooth ice cream in silence for a few minutes. Nick waved at Jamie, who was playing lawn darts with Wade and another small boy.

"What would you be doing tonight if you were at home?" Nick asked finally.

She glanced over at him.

"Just wondering what the yuppie life in California is all about," he commented with a shrug.

"Well." She lowered the hand with her cone to her knee. "Sunday night, I guess I'd be going over my Franklin, scheduling the week——"

"As in Delano Roosevelt, or as in the turtle guy on *Nickelodeon?*"

"What?"

"Who. Who's Franklin?"

"A Franklin's a planner. An object, not a who." She thought everyone knew that. She couldn't help laughing. "You interrupted me."

"Just getting it straight."

"Got it now?"

"Us corn-fed boys take a while to catch on."

"Are you mocking me?"

"So you'd be planning your week. What else?"

"Well, Franklin and I would probably send a few e-mails, make a list of calls for my assistant for the next day, maybe do a little online research."

"What's your assistant's name?"

He *had* been her assistant, anyway. "Brad."

"And Brad's a person, right?"

"Of course Brad's a person. What else?"

"I don't know." He gave his cone a lick and cast her a grin. "A companion of Franklin's maybe."

"Shut up, Nick."

His laugh warmed the cold places in her heart, places she'd deliberately neglected. He made her feel like a kid again, like she was eight years old, out of school for the summer and having the time of her life. She wouldn't have been surprised right then if he'd smashed her cone in her face and run from her with a teasing whoop.

She couldn't help herself; she laughed, too. And then something inside her, some remaining little devil from her childhood, made her reach over as he brought his cone to his lips, and give it a healthy push toward his face.

Startled, he sat with ice cream on his chin for a full minute.

Laughter and fear rose in Ryanne's chest. She knew him and yet she didn't. She hadn't done anything that impulsive in twenty years. Her heart tripped.

He turned his dark head and drilled her with a blue-eyed look of surprise and...appreciation. "Touché, you little twerp."

Ryanne smiled, the first smile she'd given him since her return.

Nick grinned, a decidedly handsome grin, even with white ice cream on his suntanned chin. With his left hand, he swiped it off and wiped it on the grass. "Remember, chicky, paybacks are hell."

Chicky? Her smile widened. "Consider me forewarned."

Lights came on around the gazebo and along the

park on all four sides. Torches were lit and, as the day waned into evening, she handed him her cone and he finished it.

Jamie came running over to where they sat. "I won two games in a row!"

"Good job," Nick replied, raising his right hand.

Jamie smacked his palm against his father's with a resounding high five.

"Did you have some ice cream?" Nick asked.

Jamie held up two fingers.

"Two?"

"Like father, like son," Ryanne said.

Jamie leaned into Nick's bare knees, and Nick turned him around and pulled him back into his lap, running a hand over his hair and clamping long fingers on his shoulder in a loving gesture. "I saw Benny Perkins's little sister over there," he said softly in Jamie's ear. "I think she wants you to come over and play tag with her."

Jamie leaned his ear away from his dad's lips and said, "Da-ad! I don't like Delores. She looks at me funny."

"That's cause she likes you. Girls get all googley-eyed like that when they like you."

Jamie jumped up and down a few times in his dad's lap, making sure he bumped him good each time his seat landed on Nick's belly. "Stop saying that."

Laughing, Nick caught him and held him still. "Okay. I'm just trying to help you out here."

Jamie turned an imploring blue gaze on Ryanne. "Tell him to stop teasing me about Delores."

Ryanne looked at Nick and said sternly, "Stop teasing him about Delores."

Nick raised both hands in surrender, and Jamie got up and ran off to play.

Ryanne couldn't get over the sight of Nick with a child. He obviously adored the boy, and the interaction between the two showed a natural loving relationship. Watching him with Jamie reminded her that even though there was still a familiar connection between herself and Nick, he was not the same boy she'd grown up with. A good many years and experiences stretched between them. A whole lifetime.

The band packed away their instruments and she watched as Birdy instructed two men on starting a hastily rigged sound system. Seconds later, recorded music floated on the night air. John Lennon's voice echoed across the lawn and bounced back from the businesses along Main Street, singing a song Ryanne hadn't heard in years—a song about starting over.

A few young couples, mostly high school age, had climbed the wooden stairs and were dancing in the shelter of the gazebo. Ryanne remembered doing that when she was a teen. She'd been on the volleyball team, the track team, in the debate club, and she'd had plenty of dates. Nick, two years younger, had preferred to hang out in his garage at home. She wondered if he'd changed after she'd left for college.

Had he danced in the gazebo? With Holly, perhaps? Curious about his marriage to the girl she remembered as Justin's girlfriend, Ryanne couldn't help wishing she knew the details.

"So, you married Holly?" she said finally.

He glanced at her, then away. "Yep."

"Didn't work out, I guess."

She fully expected an evasive "Nope," but he took

a breath and spoke. "Don't know why I ever thought it would. Foolish thinking on my part."

"Everyone thinks their marriage is going to work out, don't they?" she asked.

"Maybe two people who love each other do. At least they've got something going for them to start out with."

His reply caught her by surprise. "You didn't love her?"

He watched the dancers beneath the glowing yellow lights. "I don't know. I don't think so. And she sure as hell didn't love me."

I'm sorry, Ryanne almost said, but she didn't think he'd want her pity. "Did you *think* you loved her when you married her?"

He had pulled a blade of grass and held it between his teeth as he said, "I thought it was the right thing to do."

"For who?"

He looked at her oddly. "For everyone."

The right thing to do could mean anything. Could be they'd slept together or even that Holly had become pregnant. Ryanne held her silence and glanced toward the gazebo.

Now an eighties group she couldn't place sang about there always being something there to remind them. The nostalgic words floated over the park.

"Did you love your husband?" Nick asked.

She'd faced that internal question a hundred times recently, so she had a ready reply. "I thought I did. We had the same goals and aspirations—or so I imagined."

"Yes, you always had aspirations," he commented somewhat dryly.

She glanced at him.

He turned his head.

As their eyes met in the semidarkness, a little flicker of anger sprang to life in her. Had that been a criticism? He'd never understood her drive to succeed, and she'd never understand his contentment with things the way they were.

"At least you still have your career," he said matter-of-factly.

The anger died a quick death, replaced by hurt and embarrassment. "Oh, yes. At least I still have that."

The conversation ended as Forrest and Natalie, accompanied by Birdy and the thirty-something twins, Ashton and Elyssa Spaulding, who Ryanne learned ran the Sunshine Greenhouse, came for Nick and Ryanne and ushered them to the tables. Cold bottles of beer and wine coolers were passed around as Bruce Springsteen's caressing voice suggested dancing in the dark.

Everyone seemed warm and welcoming, greeting Ryanne and asking about her mother and her husband. Birdy blabbed that Ryanne had been divorced, and cringing, Ryanne imagined her life the fodder for gossip for the next month or more.

Pulling Ryanne aside for a moment, Birdy asked, "Do you think we could maybe get together alone one of these days? Lunch, maybe? Dinner somewhere? We don't have anywhere fancy to eat, not like the places you probably go to in California, but we could just talk. Catch up some. If you want to, that is. We don't have to." She shrugged. "No big deal."

Her hesitancy surprised Ryanne, and her apologetic tone made her uncomfortable. "Yes," she told Birdy immediately. "I'd like that. Really I would."

"You would?"

"Yes." She gave her a smile.

"Well, great then, we'll do it." Birdy gave a little wave and moved back toward the others.

Mel approached Nick. "Audrey Milligan wants a ride home, Son. And Jamie's getting tired."

Nick pulled the keys to the Chevy from his pocket. "Take her on home, Dad. And Jamie, too, if he wants to go. I'll be along in a few minutes. The freezer's already in the trunk. I'll get it out later."

Mel took the keys and wished Ryanne good-night. "Glad you came, sweetie."

"Me, too. It was fun."

Only about fifteen minutes passed before Nick asked if she was ready to go. She told those who remained good-night, and together she and Nick headed across the park toward their homes, with Madonna's voice singing suggestive lyrics behind them.

"I haven't heard those songs for ages," Ryanne said.

"Hang around Birdy enough and you will. She's stuck in the eighties."

"I'd forgotten what a great person she is."

"You lit out of here and didn't look back," he replied.

He was right about that. Ryanne hadn't spared a thought for the town or the people she'd left behind. Her sights had been set on the future, not the past. "It's been a while since I've walked this far on anything other than a treadmill,'' she said, changing the subject.

''Belong to a gym?''

''A health club, actually, but, well, I had a treadmill in my condo.''

''Had?''

''Have,'' she corrected.

''You were always running,'' he said. ''You don't run anymore?''

''Not like that.'' She'd missed it, she realized. Missed the exhilaration of the exercise and the fresh air.

They passed the business district and walked along tree-lined streets and by homes she hadn't seen in years. Some were the same, some had been remodeled. One was even gone, a drive-through bank in its place.

As they reached their street, Nick noticed Ryanne slowing down. Maybe the walk had tired her. If he thought a walk would tire him, he'd keep going until he reached Milwaukee. The scent of her hair had driven him crazy all evening. Even when he looked away, her smell invaded his senses. Damned unfair that someone so obviously not right for him could still have such a disturbing effect.

They came abreast of the Sinclair house. From the front sidewalk where they stood, the porch lights on both houses were visible, as well as the lot that stretched between, the land where Nick's vegetable garden bloomed. ''Right now there are only a few, but later in the summer, fireflies are thick through there.'' He'd certainly watched them from his window enough to know.

She said nothing.

"Remember when you cut that Morse Code alphabet from the back of a cereal box and we learned it?" he asked.

"Uh-huh."

A wave of déjà vu washed over him. "We'd signal each other at night, then sneak out and meet over there." He pointed toward the back of the lot.

"It used to be a field," she remarked, and they ambled in that direction. Now a row of houses stood where Mr. Sweeney's beans had grown.

The sharp green scent of tomato plants hung in the air here, masking her fragrance, affording him a much needed reprieve.

"Even though the trees have grown, I can still see your window from mine," he told her. "I saw the light the other night. That's why I barged over."

"I thought we were going to forget that."

"*You* were going to forget that."

She headed for her house, and he followed. She climbed the porch steps. Nick stood below, one foot on the bottom step. "Did you lock up?"

She shook her head, her hair gleaming under the porch light. A smile crooked one side of her mouth.

"Want me to come in with you? Check it out?"

"No. This is Elmwood. I'd forgotten what it was like, but I feel safe." She took another step, with him admiring her backside in her shorts, then turned back. "Thanks for taking me tonight."

"Just being neighborly."

"Night then."

"Night."

She turned, stepped into the house and closed the

door. The lock clicked. He still thought it was odd that she'd shown up out of the blue with enough boxes to make it look as though she'd moved in. Other than a holiday here and there, he couldn't remember her ever staying in Elmwood for more than a weekend. And she'd never visited when her mother wasn't here.

He headed home. The moon passed behind a cloud, temporarily casting the beanpoles and rows of thigh-high plants into blackness. Unable to resist, he glanced back and watched the light come on in the dining room window.

Inside his house, he checked the thermostat, took clothes out of the dryer, drank a glass of milk and climbed the stairs. He found Jamie enviably sound asleep, and sat in the chair beside his bed for a while, thinking how fortunate his child was to be oblivious to the world for nine or ten hours a night.

At last Nick got up and made his way to his room, where he was drawn to the window that looked out upon the Whitaker house. Ryanne's bedroom light was the only one on now, lacy curtains preventing him from seeing more than shadows when she moved. His imagination conjured up images of her removing her shorts, showering…

Once again he came to the conclusion that there wasn't much he could do to relieve his ever-present state of sexual frustration in this little town. The place was too small for casual affairs to go unnoticed, and he didn't have the time or the energy to spend on anything more. Neither did he want to subject Jamie to unstable relationships.

He'd gotten used to a good many situations in his

life that weren't his first choice; lack of sex was just another on the ever-growing list. Like lack of sleep. Lord, how he'd love to lay his weary head down on his pillow, close his eyes and have mind-numbing blackness creep over him. Sleep peacefully until he'd had his fill. He could only imagine the bliss of waking refreshed and free of the burdens that plagued his restless nights.

Yeah, right. Instead he'd become an expert on Australian football, the only programming on ESPN in the wee hours of the morning.

He glanced at the clock, figuring how many hours he had until he had a prayer of sleeping, and decided to change clothes and head out to his garage to keep his mind and his hands busy.

Around 3:00 a.m., he put his tools away, climbed the stairs and showered. With a towel wrapped around his hips, he leaned one shoulder against the window frame and scrubbed a palm over his face.

Listening to the deputies at the jail had taught him that normal people thought night ended far too soon. Not him. Not by a long shot. Night was eternal when a person couldn't sleep. Too much time to think. Too much time to regret.

He'd thought about taking up smoking, but besides being a nasty habit, it was on the list of things he shouldn't do. No caffeine, no stimulants, no alcohol before bedtime, no napping. But thinking the busyness might ease the passing of time and lessen the stress of night, he'd bought a pack, gagged on his first attempt and thrown them away. What was next? he chided himself. A bottle of Jack Daniel's to numb the ol' senses?

Nick snorted at his bleary thoughts. Sanity always fled somewhere after three in the morning. And now he had Ryanne to add to the list of things to not think about until his scheduled worrying time. He thought he'd gotten over her, but her presence, even after all these years, had the power to make him feel like a randy teenager.

And she still thought of him as a friend, a brother, something he'd resented back then, something he re-sented still.

Ryanne Whitaker still turned him inside out.

Ryanne got up early the following morning, dressed in shorts and a tank top, tied her Nikes and, after securing her hair on top of her head, headed out. She paused on the front steps to stretch, and while bending over her right leg, noticed a man in shorts walking up the front walk.

"Ryanne Davidson?"

She straightened. "Yes."

"Seems odd to deliver mail here. Your mother has everything forwarded to her. But these are in your name." He extended two envelopes.

"Yes, I had my mail sent here for a while," she replied, accepting them. "Thank you."

"Trying to beat the heat," he commented. "Un-seasonable warm, even for the Midwest."

She nodded.

"Nice to meet you," he continued, as if he had all day to stay and chat. "Name's Pat Grant."

"Nice to meet you," she replied.

"Well, stay cool."

"Sure."

He sauntered across her lawn toward the Sinclair house.

Ryanne glanced at the return addresses and tore open the envelopes. One was a check from a consignment store, where she'd left clothing to be sold, and she sighed in relief. She'd have cash for groceries and postage this week. The other piece of mail turned out to be a final bill for overdue utilities, more than she had in her bank account or her purse.

She tossed them both inside the screen door and jogged down the stairs and along the street. At the corner, she turned north and jogged toward the street behind her mother's house, checking out the new homes, with their nice lawns and two-car garages.

Continuing northward, she discovered two more blocks of homes, and then the neighborhood ended, giving way to the dusty road and cornfields she remembered.

Pacing herself, she ran as far as she thought she should and still be able to run home without killing herself, then turned back.

A car approached, and as it grew near, she moved to the side of the road. The car slowed, and she noted the sheriff's logo on the door. Wearing a brown hat with the brim shading his face, and sunglasses, the officer rolled down the window. "Morning."

She recognized Nick's voice, and then saw his lazy smile. "Morning, Officer. A renegade cow reported out here somewhere?" she asked.

"Something like that." He turned and picked up an object from the seat beside him, then handed it out the window. "You'd better wear this."

She took a step forward to accept the ball cap with

Crawford County Sheriff's Department embroidered on the front. "Thanks." She put the cap on, removed it to adjust the size, and replaced it on her head, arranging her ponytail to stick out the hole in back.

A brief glance inside the car revealed a rifle strapped to the dash, a CB radio and a clipboard. Seeing Nick in his official capacity made him seem all the more like a stranger. She took a step back. "Be careful, Matt."

He grinned and touched the brim of his hat. "Will do, Miss Kitty."

She couldn't help herself; her insides turned to liquid. She turned on her heel and jogged away, her pulse raised by more than the miles she'd run.

An odd nagging feeling compelled her to stop. Slowly, she turned back.

He was still sitting parked, watching her in the rearview mirror. All she could see of his face was his mouth and chin.

What was happening here? None of this was normal. She felt like she'd been plucked out of her life and slammed down in the middle of a Stephen King novel. "What are you looking at?"

"Your butt."

Heat rushed up her cheeks. Anger replaced the sense of displacement. Ignoring his rudeness, she turned and ran, self-conscious now.

Behind her, she finally heard the car move on.

She needed to get her life straightened out, and Nick Sinclair was messing it up. At times last evening, it had seemed as though she and Nick had picked up where they'd left off so long ago, comfortable with one another, enjoying a solid, dependable friendship.

But then something would happen—he'd give her a look, or she'd notice him anew—and she'd feel like they were strangers playing a dangerous cat and mouse game. Their friendship had evolved into unfamiliar territory. She didn't like the difference one bit.

And yet she loved it. Deep down inside, at the heart and heat of her woman's spirit, she loved this exciting, on-the-edge change.

What was wrong with her?

Chapter Five

In the heat of the day, Ryanne put the finishing touches to a change in her résumé, printed it out and read it over, trying to ignore her discomfort. She'd forgotten the stifling humidity here, so unlike the northern California weather she was accustomed to. The mugginess probably wasn't good for her computer; hadn't she heard somewhere that climate control was important? Maybe she should run the old window unit, just a little while during the afternoons. She could come up with a few dollars somewhere to pay her mom the difference in the electric bill.

Her musing was interrupted by a knock at the door. She removed her reading glasses and discovered Jamie on the front porch. "Hey, Ryanne."

"Hi, Jamie."

"I came home early today. Grampa's watching me."

"That's right, you go to summer camp."

He nodded. "Not day care."

"You're too big for day care."

He nodded again. "You got any Popsicles?"

"No. I have a couple of apples. Would you like an apple?"

"Sure."

"Come on in, and I'll wash us each one."

"Okay." He followed her through the house, curiously looking at her things spread across the dining room table. "What's all that?"

"Work."

"I thought you was taking a vacation."

"It's hard to figure out adults, isn't it?"

"Yup."

He accompanied her to the kitchen, where she washed two pieces of fruit.

"You still have my picture," he said, looking at the crayon drawing on the refrigerator door.

"Sure do. Why don't we sit on the front porch? It's shady there."

"It's hot in your house."

"Don't I know it." They sat on opposite ends of the wide banister, their backs up against the columns, their feet in front of them, hers bare, Jamie's in blue tennis shoes with an animated race car on the sides. "What's that on your shoes?"

Jamie chewed a bite and swallowed. "That's *Super Sprint.*"

"Is it a cartoon character?"

"No, it's a TV show."

"Oh." She was so far removed from children's

television, she had no idea what he was talking about. "Ever heard of Fat Albert?"

"No." He took a bite that crunched loudly. "Does he live in Elmwood?"

She stifled a giggle. "No. He was in a cartoon when I was a kid."

"Oh. That was a pretty long time ago. I don't think they show that anymore."

Wounded, she conceded, "Probably not."

"My dad said they showed Scooby-Doo when he was a kid, though."

"Yes! Do they still show that?"

"Yup. On *Nickelodeon.* I got a beach towel and a tent of Scooby-Doo."

"Wow. Your dad and I used to set up a tent. Sometimes we even slept in it for a night."

"Really? Cool!"

"Well, we started out in the tent, but we never really made it the whole night. One of us always wanted to quit and go home before we ever fell asleep."

"Were you scared?"

"Kind of. Back there where those houses are now used to be fields. At night it was pitch-dark, with no light except the moon and stars."

After they'd finished their fruit, they saw who could throw their core the farthest, and Jamie won, declaring he got his right under the maple tree where the blue jays would come down and eat it.

They sat in the grass for a while, waiting for a bird to show up, but the birds were smart enough to stay out of the heat. Jamie studied the ants crawling over the apple core and wanted to find the anthill they'd come from. Ryanne was crawling through the grass with her butt in the air when a deep voice startled her.

"Only so much of that a man can stand in a day."

Abruptly she sat on the object of his attention, finding Nick towering over them, still in his uniform, hat and black sunglasses. The automatic she'd seen up close and personal the night of her return rode in a holster on his hip.

"Dad!" Jamie jumped up and ran to give his father a boisterous greeting. Nick knelt and opened his arms. The hat flew backward, the sunglasses dislodged and fell to the grass, and Nick landed on his rump, laughing. "Handcuff me, Dad!"

Nick obliged by snapping silver handcuffs around Jamie's slender wrists, but the child immediately slipped them off and made an escape, running around Nick and giggling. Nick caught him and fastened the cuffs around his ankles. Jamie tried to walk, falling repeatedly and laughing.

"So," Nick said to her, rising to his knees, the fabric of his uniform pants stretched taut across his thighs, "what were you do doing crawling around on the grass?"

"Looking for an anthill, of course."

"Of course."

"Dad, do you know Fat Albert?" Jamie asked.

"How old do you think I am?" his father replied. "I'm not old enough to remember that."

"You are so," Ryanne said.

"Ryanne remembers," Jamie told him.

"Well, Ryanne's *older* than I am," he said with a teasing emphasis on the word *older*.

"How would you like a family of ants stuffed up your nose?" she asked.

Jamie whooped with delight at that, tried to stand and tripped.

"If you think you're big enough," Nick said, daring her by flaring his nostrils. Both hands rested on his thighs. "Come on."

She got to her feet and brushed grass from her knees.

Nick's heated regard climbed the length of her legs, lingered on her breasts and finally met her eyes. An aching heat pooled in her chest and spread rousing warmth through her body. "I *do* think you're big enough," he declared in a seductively low voice.

Flustered, she avoided his scrutiny and hated the heat creeping up her body to her face.

Jamie crawled to the apple core and reported, "There's a hundred here! Are you really gonna try to put them in my dad's nose?"

"No," she replied. "I think there's a city ordinance preventing cruelty to—insects."

Jamie looked to his father. "Is there really, Dad?"

"I'm not sure, Jamie. I work for the county, not the city. I'd have to check into that. For now, we'd better go see your grandpa and scrounge up something for supper."

"Can we have hot dogs?"

"Again?" At Jamie's nod of certainty, he said, "You can have a hot dog. I think Grandpa and I'll have something we can sink our teeth into."

"Steak?"

"You want those cuffs off yet?"

"Yeah. Thanks for playin' with me," Jamie said to Ryanne. "Maybe I can come back tomorrow."

"That would be great."

"Wanna have supper with us?" Nick asked over his shoulder as he took a key and released Jamie.

"Oh, no thanks. I planned something light."

"Three steaks is as easy as two," he coaxed, standing to his full height.

"Come on," Jamie begged. "I can show you my new *Super Sprint* video."

She met Nick's blue-eyed regard. "You wouldn't want to miss that, would you?" he asked.

"Well…"

"Please?" Jamie asked, turning imploring Nicklike eyes on her. "You can see my Scooby-Doo tent, too."

"Okay," she said. "I need to go shut down my computer."

Half an hour later, she sat in the Sinclairs' family room, a strictly masculine domain featuring a black leather sofa and recliners, a wide screen TV and functional tables and lamps. The walls were decorated only by photographs of Jamie, framed drawings—obviously Jamie's handiwork—and certificates.

Jamie played a video for her and showed her a case filled with small collector cars. "This one's like my dad's," he said, and drove the Chevy with sharp tail fins across the top of a trunk that served as a coffee table.

"It sure is."

"Guess where I got this one," he said, holding up an apple-red truck.

"Um. Santa brought it to you."

He scoffed. "There's no Santa, Ryanne. Only babies think there's Santa."

"Sorry. Your dad bought it for you," she guessed again.

"Nope. My friend Wade traded it to me for my silver one with the black stripes."

"Ah-ha." Ryanne admired his car collection for several minutes, until Nick invited her to join him in the kitchen.

"I figured you'd be grilling outside," she said, watching him turn steaks on the grill built into the countertop stove. The smell of cooking beef made her mouth water.

"Too hot. Want to slice that tomato?"

She picked up the tomato and a knife and did as he'd asked.

Mel stood across the center island from her, tearing salad greens. "Sure is nice to have you back," he said. "Are you enjoying your vacation?"

Thinking over her day, as well as the evening before, she realized these had been some of the best, most relaxing times she'd spent in years. She hadn't thought of—her stomach took a plunge—Mason all day. Quickly she detoured the direction of her thoughts. "I think I am. My calves are a little sore. I ran a couple of miles this morning."

"In this heat? Ah, well, you're young."

Nick reached back for a plate, his gaze sliding across her and a smile inching one side of his mouth into a self-amused grin. Recalling his comments about her being older than him, she wondered if that's what he was thinking. When Mel turned toward the sink, she flicked the tomato stem she'd cut out and it hit Nick in the neck.

He had changed out of his uniform into a T-shirt and worn jeans. The soft-looking shirt emphasized his broad shoulders and well-formed back. When he reached up to remove the bit of tomato from his neck, his muscles flexed with the movement, and her mouth went dry.

He forked the delicious-looking steaks onto a plate.

They ate informally in the breakfast nook, Jamie chattering about his day, about the games he and Ryanne had played that afternoon. Being around Jamie was like being around Nick a hundred years ago. Nick had always been full of energy and quick to laugh. That playfulness had been stifled when his mother had taken ill. Ryanne remembered him always working and taking care of Justin during those difficult years.

Sometimes now, in the little things he said, the teasing looks he gave her, she glimpsed the Nick she'd known back then. He looked so good to her, so surprisingly good, that until now she hadn't noticed the tired lines around his mouth. When her focus settled on his lips, and she found herself watching him chew, she dragged her attention back to her food.

She hadn't eaten a steak this good—or a steak, period—for six months, and she enjoyed every savory bite until she couldn't take another.

"You done?" Nick asked.

She nodded, and he stabbed the remainder, placed it on his plate and cut into the beef.

Ryanne ran her finger down the condensation on the tall glass of ice water Nick had poured for her.

Taking a drink, she glanced up to find him studying her with blue fire in his eyes. She set the glass down, swallowing and blotting her lips with her napkin.

Nick laid down his fork.

Something odd was happening between them, something unfamiliar and disturbing. It was as though a subtle, yet forceful current ran between them, channeling energy back and forth.

"Do we get dessert?" Jamie asked, after polishing off his second hot dog.

Nick tore his gaze from Ryanne's and nodded. "Strawberry shortcake."

"Yippee!"

"You made it?" she asked, prepared to be impressed again.

In reply, he whispered, "I bought it at Turner's deli. Norm has a gal come in and make desserts and salads each day. Don't blow my image. The kid thinks I'm super dad."

"Your image is safe with me."

He gave her a wink and stood to clear the plates.

She raised a hand, and he sat back down. "Let me," she offered.

Carrying dishes to the sink, she arranged them in the dishwasher, then found the dessert in the refrigerator. Single slices, four of them. "How did you know I'd be having dinner with you?"

"I didn't."

"One piece was for your lunch tomorrow," she guessed.

He shook his head. "Midnight snack."

"Good thing I saved you. You'll get fat, waking up to eat at midnight." She wasn't kidding anybody.

He looked great, so whatever he'd been eating thus far had been in his favor.

"Nick's already up at midnight," Mel said. "He's a night owl."

Could have fooled her. He looked as though he'd gotten his beauty sleep in spades.

"You didn't get to see my tent yet," Jamie said, finishing his dessert and jumping up.

"Wash your hands, Son," Nick told him automatically.

"Yes, sir." Jamie went into a bathroom off the kitchen and water ran for several minutes.

"He's a thorough washer," Nick explained.

Ryanne nodded.

"There's also a pump bottle of glittery blue soap in there. Smells like bubble gum," Mel said, wrinkling his nose. "And Nick finally got him washing his hands without kicking up a fuss."

Jamie returned, smelling like Double Bubble, and led Ryanne up the stairs to his bedroom.

He had a bed that looked like a race car, with a matching spread and pillows and curtains. One entire wall held shelves four feet tall, which were stuffed with action figures, cars and trucks of all sizes, videos, crates of blocks and cans of Lego, balls and board games. Jamie opened a closet that held more toys, as well as clothing and plastic storage containers, and pulled out a vinyl tent, which he promptly pulled open and snapped into form.

Scuttling inside, he called, "Come on in. It's really cool."

Cool was the right word. Being in the Sinclairs' house was the first time she hadn't perspired buckets all day. Ryanne crawled in and imagined lying down for a long comfortable nap. Jamie immediately scrambled out, and returned with a plastic Scooby-Doo lunch box.

"Those were made of metal when I was a kid."

"I know. Wade's dad collects 'em. He has some really cool ones, like GI Joe and the Porridge Family."

"The Partridge Family?"

"Uh-huh. This one's not for lunch, though. This is for my special stuff."

"Oh."

"Wanna see?"

"If you want to show me."

He opened the latch and solemnly removed a stack of photographs, their corners bent and worn. He showed her a picture of Nick and another man standing beside a small car that she'd seen but couldn't place. "What kind of car is this?" she asked, more to herself than to the child.

But surprisingly, he knew the answer. "A VW Carmen Ghia," he replied.

Nick had a dark beard and she had to look twice to make sure it was him.

The next snapshot was of Jamie at a birthday party, surrounded by gifts and balloons. Another showed him blowing out five candles. Yet another had him sprawled on Mel's lap in one of the leather recliners, both of them sleeping. She smiled.

"This is me and my mama," Jamie told her, reverently extending a picture.

Ryanne took it and studied the frail-looking blonde holding the chubby, dark-haired baby. The young woman's smile seemed kind of sad. Ryanne remembered Holly with Justin, two teenagers laughing, holding hands, driving fast. She tried to picture Nick with this girl, married to her, making love to her, but she couldn't.

"She's pretty, isn't she?"

"Very pretty." Ryanne hadn't been around many kids, but Jamie seemed like a smart, friendly, well-adjusted child, even though he'd obviously missed having a mother. Even after observing the Sinclairs for only a few days, she knew without a doubt that Nick had done a terrific job of raising his son.

"Will you read me a story?" he asked.

"Jamie, don't walk all over Ryanne." Nick's voice came from above the tent.

The child met her eyes, a question in his.

She smiled indulgently. "I don't mind reading him a story. In fact, let me go get the falcon book your grandma gave me."

"All right!"

Nick's hair-sprinkled feet, still bare as they'd been as he'd cooked supper, were the first things she saw when she crawled out of the tent. She stood up and faced him.

"If you're sure, I'll go take a shower," he said.

"Go ahead. I'll be right back, Jamie."

When she returned, Jamie had spread a blanket and piled his bed pillows inside the colorful plastic tent. Ryanne crawled in and made herself comfortable. The boy had even angled the lamp beside his bed so that the light shone directly through a flap on the side. He wore a pair of summer pajamas and smelled like bubble gum and toothpaste. Maybe it was bubble gum toothpaste.

As soon as she opened the book, he scooted over beside her, his shoulder against her arm, his hip against hers, and it was the most natural thing in the world to slip her arm around him.

There'd never been a child in her life, and the feelings this little guy created inside her were new. What a loving, trusting creature he was. Inquisitive, bright. And unique. Even though he reminded her of Nick, he was his own person, a person she'd begun to like very much.

Occasionally, Jamie made a comment about the story or asked a question. When it was over, he pulled a comic book from under the blanket and showed her the pictures, making up delightful captions as he turned pages.

Finally, he laid the comic down and rolled over with his cheek against a pillow. His eyelids lowered drowsily. "My dad's gonna build me a tree house for my next birthday. It's gonna be in the tree beside the garage."

"That's a good tree."

"It has a place where sticky stuff comes out," he mentioned. "You should see it."

"That's sap."

"Oh. What's it for?"

"Well…I guess the sap in a tree is like blood in our bodies. It probably carries the nutrients out of the soil up into the branches, like our blood carries vitamins and minerals from our food to all parts of our bodies."

She wasn't sure her explanation was scientifically

correct, but it didn't matter, because his eyes had drifted shut and he'd fallen asleep.

Hesitantly, Ryanne touched his silky dark hair, fingered it back from his temple, placed the backs of her fingers against his incredibly smooth cheek and caressed the skin for a moment. Nick was a lucky man, and any mother who could leave this child was a woman she didn't understand. But then, she didn't know the circumstances, and she wasn't anyone who should be criticizing others on their choices.

She moved the books to the side and covered him with the end of the blanket, then backed out of the tent and turned off the lamp.

Nick was downstairs at the computer, studying numbers and listings of some sort on the screen. He caught her approach from his side vision. "Shall I go up and tuck him in?"

"Too late. He's out. Inside the tent."

He grinned. "You'll be his favorite playmate if you don't say no once in a while."

"I didn't mind." She hadn't had anything better to do, really, and being with Jamie made her forget about her weighty problems for a while. She hadn't been able to do that for months, so their time together that day had been a blessing. "What are you doing?"

"Comparing prices on some parts."

Standing behind him, she breathed in the enticing scent of sandalwood—his soap or shampoo. "Car parts?"

"No, body parts. I have a black market thing going on here. Don't look in the freezer."

His short, dark hair was still wet. "You're still a smart-ass, Sinclair, you know that?"

"Yeah."

"Where's your dad?"

"Watching TV in his room." He bookmarked a site and signed off, turning toward Ryanne in the chair.

"You have a great kid," she told him, backing away and leaning against the center island counter.

He had dressed in a pair of faded jeans with a rip in one knee and a T-shirt with the armholes cut out nearly to his waist, exposing acres of tanned skin. He nodded in agreement.

"I didn't mean to interrupt you," she said, gesturing to the computer.

"I have all night," he replied.

She raised a brow. "Like you don't need to sleep?"

He shrugged. "Care for an iced tea?"

"I'd better get going."

"Jamie enjoyed you spending time with him. Thanks."

"No need to thank me. I enjoy him, too."

"He doesn't get to spend much time with, well, women, except at his day care. I know they're great to him and love him, but there are a dozen kids there, and he probably feels a lot more special having you all to himself."

"He is special, Nick. I never knew that a child would be…fun."

"It's not all fun, trust me."

"I suppose not." She headed for the back door, and he followed.

The muggy night air enveloped her as she stepped onto the back porch. He closed the door behind him and glanced upward. "Look at that clear sky. There are a million stars tonight."

They stood side by side in the backyard, necks craned. "I can't remember the last time I did any star gazing," she said. "I guess I'd see them once in a while from the balcony of my condo, but it wasn't like this. The lights of the city outshine the stars. Here, you can see all of heaven."

"If I didn't know you better, I'd think you've missed this place."

"No. I didn't miss everybody knowing about and butting into my business. I didn't miss the dreadful winters." She lowered her gaze to study her mother's house. She hadn't missed the monotony or the provincial amenities. "How have you stood it this long?"

The question didn't surprise Nick. Ryanne had always wanted to leave Elmwood. She'd never understood his lack of desire to get away. He recalled one time, the year she'd been a senior and he'd been a sophomore, when she'd spoken to him of how she was going to take her scholarship and make something of herself in the world.

"Don't you want to do something more than just work on old cars?" she'd asked him. *"What have you planned for after high school?"*

Working on old cars had sounded just fine to him. Still did. But she'd made it plain that his aspirations weren't lofty enough for her. Obviously, she thought the same of his lowly sheriff's job.

"Where would I go that would be better than here?" he asked, honestly wondering. "The things that are wrong in my life would still be wrong no matter where I went. And many of the things that are good would be left behind.''

She contemplated him, as though absorbing his words, but he knew she didn't comprehend his hometown philosophies. ''Haven't you ever · wanted more?'' she asked.

She had no idea. She knew nothing about him. Not really. Sure, he'd had dreams—who didn't? But he'd had responsibilities, too. Still did. Her question angered him. ''Do you think you're happier than I am because you went after more?'' he asked.

She sucked in a breath and looked away quickly.

''Is more all it's cracked up to be?'' he persisted.

She shrugged a shoulder finally. ''I'd better go in.''

She took a step to move away, but he caught her wrist.

Turning back slowly, she glanced up at his face. Moonlight accentuated the moisture glistening in her eyes. He was an idiot. He hadn't meant to hurt her. ''Hey,'' he said. ''I'm proud of you for making something of yourself.''

''Don't be,'' she replied.

He dropped his hand from her arm. ''Let's walk down around the corner and see if we can spot any muskrats in the creek.''

''What about Jamie?''

''He's fine. Dad's still awake.''

Surprising him, she said, ''Okay.''

They walked across his backyard, down a block and cut across a steep bank that led down to Penny Creek. The grass was high, and he walked ahead of her, flattening a path. Beneath his bare feet, the grass was cool. Near the water's edge, they stopped and studied the bubbling water as it flowed over rocks and limbs in the moonlight.

"Remember when we thought we'd catch one?" he asked. "We made a trap out of my dad's tomato cages and some chicken wire."

Ryanne laughed and found a flat rock to sit on.

Nick sat beside her.

"I remember we sat along this bank and discussed how Mrs. Kingsley got a baby in her stomach."

He nodded.

"I was right," she told him. "I knew from the girls in gym class that it had something to do with taking all your clothes off."

He laughed out loud. "I *so* did not want that to be the truth. I could not picture my parents together with their clothes off. Shame on you. There you were, the older one, filling my head with sex talk."

"Yeah, well, you're the one who told me about condoms."

"That wasn't until seventh grade, and you were in ninth. I just wanted to make sure you didn't do anything stupid."

"Not likely."

"Meaning?"

"Meaning, I never did more than *kiss* a boy until college."

"Seriously?"

She nodded.

"Then what did you do in college?"

She shook her head and made a motion of waving him away. "Oh, no. You're not getting any sex stories from me."

"So you had sex?"

"No! Well, I... Shut up."

"So you didn't even have sex in college," he surmised, pleased with himself for pulling it out of her, and pleased with the information for some reason. "You were too busy cracking the books, weren't you?"

"There's nothing wrong with that." Her chin came up.

"You're right."

"What about you?" she asked.

"What about me?"

"How old were you?"

"Twenty-one." He turned his head to catch her reaction, if any.

She was studying him with a frown. "But wasn't that about when you got married?"

He nodded.

"Oh wow," she said, taking a breath.

"What?"

"You saved yourself for marriage?"

"Not exactly. I just didn't...there wasn't anyone— anybody—I wanted to get involved with."

"Until Holly."

"Until Holly," he agreed.

"And what about after Holly?" she asked. "Still saving yourself?"

"You're getting kind of personal here."

"You started it."

She amused him more than she could know. This was so like the conversations they'd had all their lives. So different from anything he'd ever shared with anyone else. And he didn't mind the intimacy one bit. "I've dated a few women since Holly."

"Dated?"

"You know."

"Really? Ha! Who?"

He stood up at that. "I'm not going to tell you who!"

"Why not? Are you ashamed?"

"No!"

"Embarrassed?"

"No."

"What then?"

"Well, you just don't need to know," he said finally. He moved to the edge of the water, used his toe to find a rock, and threw it into the creek.

"Okay," she said from behind him.

Another splash sounded.

"'Spose that was a frog?" she asked.

"Maybe."

They listened in companionable silence.

"Birdy?" she asked softly.

It took a minute to figure out what the question was, and when it dawned on him Ryanne was still questioning him about his sexual partners, he turned to her. "No!"

She found a rock and threw it herself. "Good."

That stumped him. "Why?"

"Just wouldn't want to picture you and Birdy, that's all. I'm supposed to be having lunch with her soon."

"And thinking about that would spoil your appetite? Gee, thanks."

"No," she said, humor in her voice. She was standing higher than him, and reached out to place her hand on his shoulder. "Let's drop it."

As an instinctive reaction, he raised his hand and wrapped his fingers around her wrist. Beneath his touch her bones were delicate, her skin soft. She wore a light powdery fragrance that wasn't overpowering or flowery, and he liked it on her.

That same electrical current that had passed between them earlier arced now, and their easy camaraderie vanished, replaced by a tension so thick and tangible he found it difficult to draw a breath.

"Nick," she whispered, almost a question, almost a caress.

She raised her free hand and touched one fingertip to the corner of his mouth.

This was Rye, his friend. This was a desirable, sexy woman whose touch set him on fire. He couldn't remember ever wanting anything as badly as he wanted to kiss her right then. She was right. He did want more.

So he did exactly what he shouldn't do. He pulled her wrist toward him, and when she leaned forward, he wrapped his other arm around her waist, drew her against him and covered her lips with his.

Chapter Six

Ryanne was so surprised that she couldn't think right away. And when her thoughts did slide into focus, she realized she was standing on the creek bank—one hand on Nick's shoulder, the other fisted in the air—kissing him. A dizzying quiver ran along her brain stem and turned her insides to jelly.

She shouldn't be doing this—*they* shouldn't be doing this. This was Nick, and this just wasn't right.

All the contradictory feelings she'd had for him—all the looks he'd given her, the remarks he'd made—flowed into place and made it clear that this moment was what all that had been leading toward.

His lips were warm and full and gentle, his strong arm against her back a solid support, not a restraint. She moved her hand from the soft knit of his shirt to the side of his neck and spread her fingers over the warm solid flesh, finding his short silky hair with her fingertips.

Bringing her other hand up, needing to hang on, to touch him, she found the gaping sleeve of his shirt and slid her palm beneath the fabric and across his warm, sleek-skinned shoulder.

At her touch, he drew in a breath, barely breaking the contact of their lips. It was enough separation to make her experience the acute loss, and to be relieved when he circled her with his other arm and drew her closer. As one, their lips fused and the kiss took on more heat, more intensity. Ryanne could barely think for the exhilaratingly sensuous feelings his mouth and his nearness were creating in her. She skimmed her palm down his shoulder blade, his skin a titillating caress to her newly awakened perception.

Without conscious consent, she gave herself over to the pureness of taste and senses, taking oblivious pleasure in an entirely new, entirely exotic happening. Oh sweet heaven, the man could kiss. He plied her mouth with prolonged sweetness, nipped the edge of her lower lip, plucked and pursed and played until her head grew light and her body heavy.

Nick brought both hands up to the sides of her head, leaving her clinging to him for support, and cupped her face, ran a thumb over her jaw, then forced her away to look into her eyes.

Ryanne raised her eyelids as though drugged. In the moonlight, she noted the sheen of his dark hair, the heat in his gaze...the night air cooling her lips. She licked them once, tasting him. Wanting him.

This time when he lowered his head, the touch of his lips was familiar, like a caress she'd missed and longed for. It was easy to lose herself, to close off reality and simply indulge.

And that's what kissing Nick was like, an indulgence…like a calorie-laden, hot fudge sundae with whipped cream and red, ripe strawberries. Like the most pleasurable thing imaginable…a forbidden delicacy that wouldn't be regretted until later.

She leaned into him, then urgently groped for his wrists and brought his hands up over her breasts. He broke the kiss. They stood that way, Ryanne's eyes closed tightly, her lower lip caught between her teeth, pressing against his hands as he cupped her breasts in his palms and kneaded.

Nick had lost all reason. The urgent—almost pained—expression on Ryanne's lovely face, the feel of her soft full breasts, everything about this unexpected encounter had him aroused to a fever pitch. This hungry need for her took his breath away, robbed him of his common sense. He recognized it, and knew better. But right at this moment—this erotic, mind-numbing moment—he didn't care.

He'd always felt something special for her. But the feelings had been tender. Innocent.

These primal urges were anything but innocent. He wanted to strip Ryanne's clothes from her sexy little body and satisfy himself in her right here and now. And the most frightening realization of all at this moment was that she seemed all too willing to comply.

He tested his theory by running his thumbs over the tight buds of her nipples. She sucked in a breath and her body trembled. Her breath caught in feathery little hiccups. *Mercy!*

He remembered what she looked like in those

skimpy panties, and swallowed hard. "Rye?" he said softly.

Her eyes fluttered open. In the moonlight, her brow furrowed in a questioning frown.

"What are we doing?" he asked, his voice sounding ragged to his ears. When he heard it, his brain was jogged into a moment of lucidity. This was the girl who couldn't wait to leave for greener pastures, the woman who had aspirations and dreams that didn't include him or his obligations. If he could have sex with her without getting his head involved, he might think about it, but he knew how he'd felt about her before. And he wasn't up to subjecting himself to her desertion once again. "What the hell are we doing?" he asked again.

This time he released her and backed away.

After swaying in the darkness, she caught her balance as though orienting herself. She stuck the fingers of one hand in her hair, pulling it away from her face, and stared at him, her eyes wide. "Oh my…"

"We are going to forget that," he said, and turned away to stare at the creek.

She didn't say anything. The frogs had begun a cadence that filled the silent void.

Finally, her trembling voice reached him. "I want to be friends, Nick."

She'd always wanted to be friends. He almost laughed at the futility of getting himself mixed up with her again. "I know."

"I'll forget if you will."

Like there was a chance in hell of that. "Okay."

"I'm going home."

"I'll be right behind you."

The grass swished and she moved away. Nick turned and watched her walking up the bank. After a moment, he followed, staying behind her as she hurried through the neighborhood and reached her mom's place.

She entered the house and closed the door. Nick sat on a bench on his back deck and watched the downstairs lights go out and another come on in her bedroom.

What disturbed him in addition to being more frustrated than ever was the fact that she'd have done it. He really believed she would have had sex with him, taken a moment of pleasure—heck, maybe weeks of pleasure—and then headed blissfully back to her successful, busy life.

And here he'd be. Picking up the pieces of *his* life. Going on. Existence as usual. Maybe he should have gone ahead. If she had no reservations, why should he? He could take care of his itch and have no added obligations, an idea that had appealed to him in theory of late.

Well, hell, maybe he still would. If the opportunity arose again.

By ten the next morning, Nick had completely vetoed the idea of another physical encounter with Ryanne. He needed to give his brain a little more control and his body a lot more space. He was sitting at his desk at the sheriff's department, reading the mail the dispatcher had opened for him, when the phone rang.

''It's Ann Marie Vincent,'' Sharon called, her hand

over the mouthpiece. "Eddie's at it again. Want Bryce to take it?"

Nick stood. "No, tell her I'm on my way."

He grabbed his hat and headed for the door.

Five minutes later, he was driving up the graveled lane to the Vincent place, a small house with peeling paint that sat on an acre of land. Ann Marie worked afternoons and evenings at the Three B's Bar; her husband, Eddie, worked nights at the nearby soybean plant. Their only child, a son, would be a fifth grader at Elmwood Elementary when school started in the fall.

Nick had been to this house too many times to count. He parked and ran up the cracked walk. Through the screen door, he could hear the man shouting. Without bothering to knock, he yanked open the door. "Ann Marie! Eddie!"

The living room appeared unscathed, the worn carpet, upholstery and spindly-legged tables looking as pathetic as always, the portable television tuned to a game show. "Did you call him?" Eddie's angry voice rang from the kitchen.

Nick strode toward the sound, his gut clenching with apprehension at what he might see. The first sight that met his eyes was food strewn across the floor and streaked, as though it had been walked through. A pork chop lay under the edge of one counter, peas smashed everywhere.

Ann Marie was sitting at the table, her head buried in her hands, her dark hair covering her face. Eddie, obviously drunk, told her to shut up, and stared at Nick with glaring defiance. "You can get the hell out of my house," he said.

Nick crossed the room. "Ann Marie, are you all right?"

She didn't look up.

He placed a hand on her shoulder, and she flinched, then tossed her hair back and looked up at him, shame and grief and hopelessness prominent in her glistening eyes. The corner of one and her cheekbone were turning black and blue, and a trickle of blood ran from the corner of her dry, cracked lip.

Helplessness and anger washed over Nick in a nauseating wave, and he tamped down the emotions to let the lawman in him take over.

"I'm all right," she said. "Just take him in to cool off for a while."

Eddie threw a plate across the room and it crashed against the doorjamb. "I wouldn't need to cool off if you'd learn to fix me a decent meal! I work all night long and I come home to leftovers! A man has to eat to stay alive! How the hell do you think the bills get paid around here?"

"Yeah, well, I work, too, Eddie," she said tiredly. "It's not exactly a picnic at the Three B's, no matter what you think. And I don't get any help around here."

"How do you think other women do it?" Eddie asked. "Other women work and still fix decent meals."

"Maybe their husbands don't spend the grocery money on booze!"

"I got a right to relax!" he shouted, and stomped toward the table, slipping on the mashed peas and lurching forward.

Nick shot out a hand and restrained him. "Back off, Eddie."

"She's mouthy, you hear that?" he shouted, catching his balance. "The bitch deserves everything she gets."

"No, she doesn't." Nick still held him by a shoulder. "Nobody deserves to get hit for voicing an opinion."

"She never had an opinion worth wastin' breath on." Jerking from Nick's grasp, Eddie threw open the back door and stomped out.

Nick leaned both palms on the laminated tabletop and appealed to the woman. He'd known her most of his life, had gone to school with her, and these domestic scenes made him sick. "Press charges this time. Do it for yourself. Leave. Go to your mother's. Do anything, Ann Marie, but don't stay here and let him do this to you."

"I can't take Dylan away from his friends, disrupt his life. And I can't go to my mom's. She never liked Eddie."

"Me taking Eddie in for a day isn't going to fix things, and you know it. It's like putting a bandage on a severed artery. You both need some help. Make him get it."

Ann Marie looked away. "I can't do that, Nick. He doesn't mean to get like this. He can be real sweet most of the time. It's just the alcohol."

"And that's what he needs help with. If you press charges, a judge will have him evaluated, maybe force him to go into treatment."

"It's like quitting smoking," she argued. "You have to want it before it will work. And it probably wasn't the best supper I've ever fixed him, you know?''

Nick straightened and stood with his hands on his hips in exasperation. They'd had this discussion a dozen times in the last year. He always wondered why she tried to reason with Eddie, and here Nick was, trying to reason with her. Ann Marie was right about one thing, though—she had to want Nick's help before he could give it to her. But he sure as hell didn't want to come out here and find her beaten senseless— or worse yet, dead. His hands were tied as long as she refused to take the necessary steps. ''Don't be a fool, Ann Marie.''

She stood and went to the sink. ''Thanks for coming, Nick.''

He turned and exited, finding Eddie on a stump in the overgrown weeds behind the house. ''You coming peaceably, Eddie?''

Eddie stood, teetered some and raised a hand. ''No handcuffs.''

''Okay. Get in the car.''

''Pick me up a carton of smokes tonight!'' Eddie called on his way past the kitchen window.

The sound of running water accompanied his wife's compliant, ''All right, Eddie.''

Nick shook his head, ushered his prisoner into the back of the cruiser and radioed Bryce about the situation.

After the night deputy, Duane Quinn, arrived with supper and coffee for both himself and Eddie Vincent, Nick briefed him on the events of the day and headed home.

"Dad!" Jamie met Nick as soon as he pulled into the drive.

Nick got out and knelt for a hug. "Hey, little mister."

"Dad," Jamie said, dragging him toward the house. "Me an' Wade wanna set up the big tent and camp out. Can we do that tonight?"

"Tonight?"

"Yeah. Please, Dad?"

Nick figured the boys wouldn't make it the whole night, but he'd be awake to watch them, anyway, so it didn't make much difference that it wasn't a weekend. "I guess so. Is it okay with Wade's mom and dad?"

"You can talk to them."

In the kitchen, Mel stood, stirring something on the stove. "What're you cooking, Pop?"

"Just instant potatoes to go with these here pork chops."

The image of that pork chop lying under the Vincents' counter immediately flashed through Nick's mind and he shoved it aside. "Sounds good. I'll change and set the table. We have salad greens from yesterday. I need to get out there and pull radishes."

Upstairs, he washed, changed into jeans and a T-shirt and glanced out the window. Ryanne was sitting on her shady front porch with a book, her bare feet propped on the banister. Why should he deny himself something with the possibility of being so good, just because it couldn't be permanent? No one would have to know, she'd be gone soon and there'd be no strings, no messy relationship hassle. What would be the harm? People did it all the time. For the tenth time that day, he changed his mind.

After supper, Nick told his dad to leave the dishes, and he and Jamie brought a tent from the garage and laid it out on the grass in the backyard.

"It smells funny, Dad."

"Needs some air is all. You usually want to let 'em stand a day or so after they've been stored."

Mel had come out to watch from a lawn chair, and a few minutes later, Natalie Perry dropped off Wade. The excited boys proved to be more hindrance than help, as they asked questions and used the stakes in a sword fight. They ran toward the Whitaker house and returned with Ryanne in tow.

"Want a hand?" she asked.

Nick glanced at her curvy shape in navy jogging shorts and a sleeveless white top. Instantly, the remembered feel of her breasts in his hands had him looking away and taking a calming breath. "Sure."

With her help, the tent went up quickly. "There are cots in our basement," she said. "I saw them the other day."

"Can we use 'em?" Jamie asked.

"Of course," she agreed. "Why don't you boys come help me carry them?"

Nick couldn't help turning his head to watch her walk away, Jamie and Wade jogging along on either side.

"She's really something, isn't she?" Mel remarked.

Nick tied up a canvas window flap. "That she is."

"The air-conditioners working okay over there?

The girl never uses 'em. Evelyn never did put in central air. Shame she didn't.''

''As far as I know, they work fine,'' Nick replied. He had wondered the same thing about Ryanne not running the window units. Maybe the humidity just didn't bother her, but he couldn't imagine that being so.

A sound sidetracked him, and he glanced over to see Ryanne using a handheld vacuum on two aluminum frame cots. She helped the boys carry them over, and Nick set them up inside.

''Now we gotta get all our stuff,'' Jamie said, and he and Wade galloped indoors.

''Nick's a dad like you,'' Ryanne said to Mel, and from inside the tent, Nick overheard the comment. He glanced out the net window opening. She nestled down on the lawn in front of his father's chair. ''My dad never did fun things with us.''

''He was a busy man,'' Mel replied.

''So were you. But even later, when your wife was ill, you had time for your boys.''

Mel said nothing, but laid his hand on Ryanne's shoulder. She turned her head to smile at him, and Nick's chest hurt at the sight. He bent at the waist to exit the tent opening, and busied himself with picking up the bags and his hammer.

''Do you remember when Justin set off that bottle rocket and it caught my mom's clean sheets on fire on the clothesline?'' Ryanne asked.

Mel groaned, but she laughed.

She continued. ''How about when he poured gas down that hole in the yard and threw in a match to get rid of the snakes?''

Mel shook his head. "That boy didn't have eyebrows or eyelashes for months."

Listening to them reminisce, a person would think Justin's antics had all been harmless and amusing, but they hadn't been. He'd been in trouble time and again, and it had always been Nick getting him out of scrapes. The older Justin had gotten, the more serious the incidents, until he and Nick had been at odds all the time. Nick grabbed his tools and headed for the garage to put them away.

Ryanne rearranged herself on the grass to watch Nick stomp away. "It bothers him to hear us talk about Justin?" she asked.

Mel shrugged. "He never talks about his brother." He stood and glanced at his watch. "I'll be heading in. Time for my TV show."

Ryanne got up and followed the path Nick had taken, finding him replacing tools on an orderly pegboard inside the gigantic garage. Two draped cars were unrecognizable, except for the shape of the tail fins she knew belonged to the '57 Chevy. Machinery and storage units of all kinds lined the walls.

"This looks a lot different from the garage I remember," she said, coming up beside him.

Nick wiped a clean workbench with a cloth. "It is."

"I didn't mean to upset you by talking about Justin."

He turned around, leaned back against the wood and crossed his arms over his chest. "Let's drop it then."

"Are you angry with me?"

He shook his head. She hadn't been able to think

about much besides what had happened between them last night, and she didn't want to spoil the tenuous friendship they'd resumed. She hadn't had a friend for a long time, and she was realizing what she'd missed out on. "Are you upset about last night?"

"Define upset."

"Mad?"

"No."

"Disappointed?"

His disturbing gaze locked on her mouth. "No."

Ryanne almost turned away, but at the last second, stood fast. She really didn't have anyone except her mom, who was far away, and the Sinclairs had always been part of her family. After years of independence, it was obviously a weakness to need someone like she was starting to need Nick. Maybe she could fix it—cut herself off and regroup. Or maybe she didn't want to go back to being herself—at least not just yet.

Nick lowered his arms to his sides. He pursed his lips before saying, "I had a really bad day. That's all."

"Renegade cows?"

"Something like that."

"How long do you say the boys will last in the tent?" she asked.

"Ten-thirty," he replied.

"I'll say eleven-thirty."

He raised a brow in curiosity. "What're you betting?"

She thought a minute. "I'll do your chores for a week."

He grinned. "Dishes, too?"

"Okay. And if I win?" she asked.

"You won't. I know Jamie, and he gets tired early."

"But if I do..."

"What do you want?"

She considered. Dishes wouldn't do. She needed something to alleviate the boredom. "A midnight drive every night for a week."

"Together?"

She nodded.

"Driving what?"

She gestured to the cars beneath the covers. "Yours. Mine. It doesn't matter."

"I could drive your car?" he asked.

Seemed harmless enough. "Okay."

Nick extended his hand, and Ryanne shook it, the brief contact all the warning she needed to know that whatever this thing was between them, it wasn't over yet—and she definitely hadn't forgotten the night before.

At ten-fifteen, Ryanne heard a commotion, dropped her stack of papers on the table and moved to the dining room window. Reaching back to flip off the light, she peered into the darkness toward the Sinclair house.

Someone was growling loudly...a man. Nick. He was out there trying to scare the boys! She shot across the room, through the kitchen and out the back door. "You're cheating!" she called.

Peals of childish laughter assured her the boys weren't frightened.

"You can't scare them inside!" Ryanne called "That won't count!"

From the lilac bush at the corner of his house, Nick emerged in the darkness. "That wasn't in the rules. We never said we couldn't influence them."

"I just assumed you'd play fair."

He turned a palm up.

"Okay, fine," she said, turning toward the tent. "Hey, fellas! Got anything good to eat in there?"

"Wade's mom sent some fruit gels."

"How about some popcorn? Shall I make you some popcorn?"

"Sure!"

"That'd be cool!"

"Okay, I'll be right back."

Nick followed her for a few feet. "Wait, you're keeping them awake to eat."

"You said there were no rules," she called over her shoulder.

At eleven forty-five, Ryanne waited for Nick to come downstairs after tucking in the boys.

"You cheated," Nick said from the doorway.

She made the same upraised palm gesture he had made. "So, do you start paying up tonight?"

He nodded. "Why not? Let me tell Dad I'm leaving."

He returned a minute later. "Your car or mine?"

"Yours," she replied. "Mine tomorrow."

"Okay." He grabbed a key ring from a hook by the door and ushered her outside. They entered the garage by a side door, and he pressed a button to raise the overhead door. "Give me a hand with this."

She helped loosen the cover from the edges of the bumpers and watched as another classic Chevy convertible was revealed. "Where did you get this?"

"I've had her."

"You're full of surprises, Nick."

He started the perfectly tuned engine, lowered the top and drove out of the garage. Reaching the blacktop highway a few minutes later, Nick increased speed. The wind whipped through Ryanne's hair, and looking over at her, Nick laughed.

She pointed to the CD player. "It's not eighties music, is it?" she called over the roar of the wind.

Grinning, he leaned over and pressed a few buttons. "This is a '63. What do you think?"

Martha Reeves resonated through the speakers, singing how love was like a heat wave. Of course Nick would have the appropriate music for the car. Ryanne laughed and leaned back, enjoying the ride. He drove for miles, the songs changing, the sky a panorama of stars in all directions, and Ryanne relaxed and felt better about life than she had for a long time.

Everything here was so simple, so elemental, with time to reflect and enjoy and just *be*.

Nick finally pulled over to an area on the side of the road that looked out over the river, and cut the engine. The music died, too, leaving only the sound of the water. Eventually, frogs and crickets could be heard singing their night melodies. The moon reflected off the water, a peaceful quiet scene. Ryanne leaned her head back and studied the stars.

She'd looked at the stars plenty since her return to Iowa. Before that, she couldn't remember observing the night sky since her childhood.

"Do you ever lie awake at night wondering what you're doing with your life?" she asked. "Whether or not the choices you've made have been the right ones? How different your life might have been if you'd chosen a different direction?''

Nick studied the riverbank opposite through the windshield. He'd lain awake plenty of nights—she had no idea!—but not wondering what he was doing with his life. The choice he'd made that had made all the difference had been the one to not accompany Justin the night he'd died. Every choice since then had been based on doing the right thing, taking others into consideration before himself. ''You've done what you wanted to do,'' he said. ''Gone after your dreams.''

The chirping of the frogs was the only sound for a long minute, before she spoke. ''You resent me for that, don't you?''

Chapter Seven

He couldn't answer for a minute. The perceptive question made him take a good look at what he really did feel—besides the anger and helplessness and rigid sense of obligation. "I guess I do."

She turned in the seat and faced him. "But you didn't want to leave Elmwood, Nick. Why did you care that I left?"

"You don't know what I wanted, Rye, so don't act like you do."

She blinked. "What did you want?"

He said nothing. He couldn't. Voicing regrets would be a betrayal of his love for his father and his son.

"You wanted to work on your cars," she stated. "I remember. And you've done that."

"Yes. My little hobby," he replied dryly.

She sat back in the seat and looked away.

"What are *you* regretting?" he asked. "Your marriage didn't work out. That happens to a lot of people."

"Am I supposed to feel better because I'm in the majority statistically?"

"I didn't mean that." He thought back to what she'd said about doubting her choices. He knew what a blow it was to strike out in marriage and feel like a failure. "Are you doubting your choice in a marriage partner or in your career?"

She shrugged.

"You're young and smart. You can always make changes to your career if you're not happy."

"I loved—love my job. That's not it."

"You're beautiful and sexy. You'll find the right guy."

She turned to look at him finally. "I am?" She didn't sound convinced.

"You have a mirror, Rye, and it's gotta be telling you that's one dynamite body."

"You think I'm beautiful?" she asked.

This was steering them into waters he didn't want to navigate. She'd always turned him inside out and he'd always been her brotherly confidant. Nothing had seemed to change, except for her sudden physical responses to him, and that had him confused. Was she needy for someone to make her feel desirable again—was that it? And was he the safest person available? "I think you're a knockout," he answered truthfully.

"And you liked kissing me?"

"Oh, yeah."

She sighed. "Everything's so upside down, Nick."

He agreed with a nod.

"Do you think it's dangerous?" she asked. "You know, the kissing?"

It was definitely dangerous. A major risk for his poor heart. A fatality for his sanity. He nodded again.

"Uh-huh," she said, but she'd started staring at him, her gaze moving over his shoulders and returning to his mouth. His body reacted immediately.

He closed his eyes and drew a shaky breath. This couldn't be happening. This *shouldn't* be happening, but it *was*.

"When you kiss me, Nick, I feel all those things. Beautiful, sexy, smart."

He didn't know who had leaned closer, him or her, but her breath as she spoke touched his chin. He could smell her hair, her skin, feel the warmth from her body. "You want to be friends," he reminded her, and opened his eyes.

She was looking at him like he was a gooey dessert, and he discovered it wasn't a bad feeling to be looked at like that.

"Yes, I do," she replied. "I don't want anything to ruin that. I don't want this…other thing…to ruin our friendship. What we have together is important to me."

"I guess that's a risk."

"Just tell me you won't stop being my friend."

"I won't, Rye."

"Promise."

"I promise."

She reached up and threaded her fingers into the hair behind his ear. He leaned forward, the electrical current between them pulling like a magnetic field. He kissed her mouth and she made a little sound of surprise. Drawing back to look at her, he saw no resistance or hesitation, only desire in her eyes, and the yearning look sucked his breath from his lungs as though he'd been gut punched.

He kissed her again, this time a melding of lips and tongues that spread delicious warmth through his blood and tilted his world on its axis. He knew better. He knew better! He knew squat.

He took control of the kiss, pulling her into his arms and enjoying her delicate softness against his chest. He delved his fingers into her wild sexy hair, ignoring the tangles, relishing the thick silken texture.

She touched a hand to his chest, where she must surely feel the savage beat of his heart and recognize how he felt about her. If she realized, she would pull away and laugh at him, tease him for being so serious—but she didn't.

Her reactions amazed him. Turned him on so badly he thought grimly that he'd embarrass himself at the slightest provocation.

Beneath her fingertips, Nick's accelerated heartbeat assured Ryanne that he wanted this as much as she did. She was crazy to touch him, crazy to enjoy the taste and heat and male strength of her friend. She raised the hem of his cotton shirt and let her palms glide over warm skin, satin flesh encasing hard muscles and enticing planes. When she found his chest and grazed his nipples with her fingertips, a shudder wracked his body. Newfound sexual power lent her increasing boldness.

Breaking the kiss, she shoved up his shirt, lowered her face and pressed her lips to his skin.

"You make me feel like I'm sixteen," he said with a ragged breath.

"You definitely don't feel like a sixteen-year-old to me," she replied, her smile evident in her voice, her tongue against his chest, tasting salt and man.

She had turned on the wide bench seat so that she faced him, practically sitting in his lap, and he ran his left hand up her thigh beneath the cuff of her shorts and around the back, savoring her delicate skin, touching the curve of her buttocks. Her shorts were too tight for him to reach higher, preventing a more intimate exploration, and making her wish, shamefully that she'd worn a skirt.

He grasped her backside through the fabric and caressed her in maddeningly gentle strokes.

"I can't take any more of this," he rasped against her ear. "Let's cool off."

"Then let me..." she said, reaching for the button on his jeans.

"No." He grabbed her wrist.

"Nick—"

"No. Not here. Not like this." He released her and threw open the door, jumping out of the car like it was on fire.

And maybe it was. He sure as hell was.

Facing away from her, he leaned against the fender for a good five minutes.

Ryanne closed her eyes. Unfamiliar sensations hummed through her body like liquid fire. Nick depicted every erotic fantasy she'd ever had. He made her feel like Eve, like Jezebel, like a seductress...and she liked the feeling. She felt so sexy with him she couldn't stand it. Everything about him set her aflame. Why had she never seen it—*felt* it—before?

And the fact that he wanted her as badly as she wanted him was a heady aphrodisiac. And he did. She knew it without a doubt, even if he wasn't ready to admit it yet.

Nick resorted to the sleeping pills that night—just mild ones that took the edge off and let him get enough rest so that he could function the next day. The situation was taking a toll on his mind and body. Ryanne was only here temporarily, and he wasn't convinced that their friendship could handle a brief fling.

However, fighting against his desire for her was obviously killing brain cells. The following morning, he snapped at Bryce twice and had to apologize. He ordered a carryout lunch at the Waggin' Tongue and forgot the bag on the counter. When Shirley Rumford called to him as he was getting back in the cruiser, he'd taken one look at the bag the café owner held and felt like an idiot.

"You okay, hon?" she'd asked.

"I'm fine."

"Maybe you need a little time off."

"I have a vacation coming up," he assured her.

He took his meal to the dock along the river where he used to fish, and listened for calls over the radio as he ate and had his allotted worry time. He hadn't slept well in years, but nights were worse than ever now. He was going to have to snap out of this. His mind had careened into a rut and he couldn't direct his thoughts back onto the road toward sanity.

They'd bet an entire week of midnight drives. It wasn't as if he'd have been sleeping anyway, but the sexual frustration was enough to make a man crack. Could he renege on the bet? Did he want to? God help him, no. He wanted to do exactly what they were doing. And more.

A little before 11:00 p.m. that night he called her. He'd been keeping an eye out for her lights and knew she was still downstairs. "You awake?" he asked.

"Oh, yes. It doesn't cool off enough to sleep upstairs until around one."

"Why don't you run the air?"

"It doesn't work that well when it's this hot."

"Why don't you call Nate Keenan at the hardware store? He has a repairman."

"Maybe I will."

"Are we still on?" Nick asked, thinking she might have changed her mind after she'd had time to cool off and reconsider.

"Unless you need to sleep," she said. "This wasn't very fair of me, because I know you have to go to work in the morning."

"I'm a night owl," he assured her. "Want to leave now?"

"I'll meet you in back. We're taking my car, right?"

"You said I could drive it."

"You're on."

Ryanne hung up and checked her hair in the mirror on the dining room wall. She ran a hand over her cotton top and the gauzy calf-length skirt, then picked up her purse and keys.

She could feel his appreciative gaze, even in the darkness, as she walked toward him, and she returned the admiration, taking in his long legs in faded jeans, his broad chest and ample shoulders in a gray T-shirt. Nick took the keys and unlocked the garage, spreading the aged wooden doors to each side and walking to the driver's side of her red Viper.

Ryanne opened the passenger door and got in herself—this wasn't a date, after all. She buckled her seat belt as Nick started the powerful engine and found the switch for the headlights.

She could smell him. Sandalwood and midnight air. She knew how his skin tasted. She knew the effect of his kisses on her head and her body. She knew how dangerous this game had become, but she didn't want to concede or even call for a time out. She wanted more.

Nick adjusted the driver's seat for his longer legs, tested the sensitive clutch and backed out of the drive, heading for the highway. The sound of the engine always gave her goose bumps, and from the look on Nick's face, he was experiencing the same reaction.

He gave her a sideways glance. "A hundred seventy-eight, you said?"

"That was in the middle of nowhere," she replied. "Don't even think about it."

"There's a straight four-mile stretch between the water tower here and the Cooperton Bridge," he said.

"You're the sheriff."

"Right. So, who's going to give me a ticket?"

"Not over a hundred," she warned him.

He downshifted and stepped on the accelerator. Two minutes and a near cardiac arrest later, he slowed to the speed limit. Glancing at her face, he laughed. "What? You've driven it faster."

"It's different when you're the one driving," she told him.

"What are you doing with a car like this, anyway?"

"What do you mean?"

"I'd expect you to drive a Lexus or a Beemer or something."

She didn't have time to reply, because a beeping sound interrupted.

Her first instinct was to reach for her pager, but she hadn't worn it in weeks. Nick flipped up the hem of his T-shirt and snagged the tiny phone from his waistband. "Sinclair... How long ago?" There was a longer pause. "No, I'm only about ten minutes away. Tell him to sit tight and I'll get it."

He broke the connection, and Ryanne waited to hear what was going on.

"I need to stop by the Clement place. Harold Clement thinks someone shot at his house."

"Oh my God, a drive-by shooting in *Elmwood?*"

"We don't have any gangs or anything. But this isn't the first time this has happened. I suspect someone has a grudge against Harold, for whatever reason. Probably just a kid with a rock, but I haven't found any proof. I'll drop you off at home."

"As long as you think it's safe, I don't mind riding along. It'll save you time."

"That it will."

He drove back to town and cruised up the street

where the Clement house sat. Several neighbors in varying stages of dress, from robes and slippers to sweats and bare feet, stood on Harold's lawn. Most of them turned to stare when the Viper roared to a vibrating stop at the curb.

Ryanne exchanged a look with Nick as he reached for the door. Gossip would zing along the telephone wires and at the grocery checkouts tomorrow.

Nick got out and strode toward Harold.

Ryanne leaned out the window Nick had rolled down before turning off the engine.

"Look at this, Nick," Harold said. The fifty-something pharmacist wore a plaid robe belted around his wide belly, plus white socks and slippers. What little hair he had stood on end. "Someone was shooting at our place again."

Nick studied the broken glass from the faux gas lamp that stood in their front yard. "Did you hear a shot? Could it have been a rock?"

"I heard it," Harold assured him. "Popped like a gun."

"Were there any cars? Did you see anyone drive away?"

"I looked out soon as I heard the sound." Ryanne recognized the young woman who spoke; she worked in the post office. Her name badge had read Larken.

Nick turned to the woman. "You heard it, too?"

She nodded. "I was letting my dog out."

"Did you see a car?"

"No. Nothing."

"Anyone on foot?"

She shook her head. "It was too dark and the light was behind me, from my doorway."

"A person thinks they're safe in a little town like this," Harold grumbled. "Then they get shot at. I just got this lamp fixed after the last time, too. Cost me forty-five bucks for the glass panels and the bulbs."

"Maybe the bulb just burst," Nick suggested.

"It was a shot," Harold insisted. "I know a gun-shot when I hear one."

"Well, just like last time, everybody in the neighborhood has trampled the area. If there was evidence, it's gone now," Nick told the bystanders, waving them away. "Back up, people. I'll come out first thing in the morning and look over the ground."

On her way back to her house, Larken gave Ryanne a little wave. The others headed to their homes, mumbling and giving Ryanne and her car inquisitive looks.

Nick walked Harold up to his porch and spoke with him briefly before returning to the Viper.

"Sorry about interrupting our drive." Starting the engine, he turned on the headlights.

"No problem. That kind of thing happen often?"

"Always something." He glanced in the rearview mirror and pulled onto the street.

"Tired yet?" he asked her once they were out on the highway.

Ryanne assured him she wasn't. Alone in this car with Nick, she was more awake than she'd ever been, her senses more acute, her nerve endings tingling.

He took a rutted side road, the headlights illuminating trees and the silver-red reflection of small animals' eyes along what soon became almost a dirt trail. "If I get your car dirty, I'll wash it."

She hadn't even been thinking of that. She'd been wondering where he was headed down this deserted road into darkness, and her heart had started to pound with anticipation. He knew where he was going, and eventually stopped the Viper, turning off the engine.

He switched off the headlights, and they sat in near total darkness.

"Where are we?" she asked, her breathy voice almost a whisper.

"I'll show you." He got out of the car and she followed. He took her hand and led her along a dirt path as their eyes began to adjust to the moonlight. Thick clumps of trees and shrubs eventually gave way to a clearing on the shore of a lake. Half a dozen houses stood on the opposite side, most of them dark, but a few trailing streams of yellow light across the surface of the water.

"This is a beautiful place," she said quietly.

"Cooler here, too, did you notice?" He stood close, her hand still clasped in his.

She nodded. "Who lives over there?"

"Beverly Bell lives in the one on the far right—looks like a cabin? She still owns the Three B's. A family named Murphy lives in the next one. Andy Murphy works construction projects for Jon Langley."

"How about that one?" Ryanne pointed to the home on the far left, where a dock jutted into the lake.

"Paige Duncan bought that place awhile back. She runs the pet store. Does dog grooming. Single. In her twenties."

Ryanne looked up at Nick's face. "Attractive?"

He nodded. "But not a knockout."

She smiled.

Nick stepped behind her and placed his arms

around her, hugging her gently. Leaning back into his sturdy embrace, she laid her head against his shoulder and gazed up at the stars. A gentle breeze flattened her filmy skirt against her legs. "It's peaceful here."

Nick nudged his nose against her hair, touched his lips to her ear. A shiver raced along her skin and tightened her nipples. Each second that ticked past increased the tension she was feeling inside. They both knew what they'd planned and anticipated ever since the night before, and the time had come to explore this burning attraction further.

Taking her shoulders gently, Nick turned her to face him. She favored herself with the pleasure of touching him, flattening her palms over his shirtfront, raising one finger to his chin, to the cleft in his upper lip.

Nick parted his lips and touched his tongue to her fingertip. Heat flooded Ryanne's body. The night air took on a heavy, seductive quality. The universe and all the twinkling stars in the heavens seemed to revolve around this moment, this patch of grassy bank. Ryanne and Nick were the only two people who existed right then and there, and that was as it should be. They had no past and no future, but only that moment. She stared at the longing in his expression and reveled in the fact that he felt such desire for her.

Ryanne dropped her hand to his shoulder and lifted her mouth in invitation. Nick accepted her offering immediately, lowering his head and covering her lips in a hungry, invasive kiss. She welcomed the play of his tongue as it delved and lingered and kindled the fire, which blazed hotter and hotter. Her knees grew weak with the mounting sensations, but Nick supported her weight, wrapping his arms around her.

Through her clothing, her sensitized flesh made out his hard chest and thighs, his belt buckle, as well as the pressing evidence of his arousal. Toe-curling excitement spiraled through her limbs, and she pressed closer.

Breaking the kiss, Ryanne studied him in the moonlight, amazed again that this was her old friend Nick and that she found him the sexiest man alive. He brushed the back of his curled fingers against her cheek, a decidedly adoring gesture that spoke to her needy heart. He truly found her beautiful. She smiled at the amazing fact.

Running his fingers down the bare skin of her arm, he caught her hand and raised it to his mouth, then pressed his lips against the palm. The slight roughness of his cheek against her fingertips caused her stomach to dip.

"Remember you said I make you feel like you're sixteen?" she asked.

"I remember."

"Well, I never felt like this when I was sixteen."

He chuckled. "Here I was worried about you, and you were saving yourself."

She raised her other hand and combed his short silky hair away from his temple. "In fact, I've never felt like this."

He studied her curiously. "You've never felt sixteen?"

She shook her head. "No, I've never felt… this…" She made a fist and tapped it against his chest, frustrated at the lack of words—and too embarrassed to choose any to explain. *"This,"* she said helplessly.

Nick used a knuckle to raise her chin. "I've never felt this before, either, Rye."

He understood, and that pleased her immeasurably.

He leaned over her to initiate a new kiss, and she wrapped both arms around his neck and returned it with renewed passion. Maybe she was crazy, but nothing had ever felt so good or so right. Nick made her feel good about herself, and she needed that confidence more than anything.

Running his palms up her sides, he brought them around to cup her breasts through her cotton top. Their lips parted and he swore softly. "No bra?" he questioned.

"It's hot," she breathed against his chin, but even though the night was warm, goose bumps had risen on her flesh.

Nick slid his hands under her top and found her nipples, rolling them between his thumbs and forefingers until she couldn't bear the exquisite torture. Her knees buckled.

He caught her, tilted her back while supporting her with one arm, and tasted her neck, nipped at her earlobe and darted his tongue in and out of the hollows behind her ear. All the while he continued his splendid caress of her breast.

Ryanne straightened her body and raised her knee alongside Nick's thigh. He reached down and cupped her bottom, pulling her against him, and covering her mouth with his.

She kissed him with need and longing she'd only

just discovered had been buried deep within her. She was greedy for him, for more of him.

Bunching up her skirt, he slid his palm under the fabric, found his way under her skimpy panties and stroked her bottom. The caresses grew bolder, curving under her backside.

"We could lie down here," she suggested through a heated glaze of anticipation.

"The mosquitoes would eat you alive," he replied.

"Too bad we didn't bring a bigger car," she said.

"Rye, we can't have sex right here," he told her, regret evident in his voice.

Disappointment edged into her consciousness. "Why not?"

"I don't have anything with me."

Her mind cleared enough to think. "You don't need anything."

"Why not?"

"I've had a shot. I can't get pregnant."

"Really." He straightened, loosening his hold on her and separating their bodies. Loss swept through her.

"Really," she replied.

"Don't you want to think it through?" he asked, holding her by the shoulders now.

"No. No, I don't." She straightened her skirt, avoiding his eyes, acutely uncomfortable talking about this now that he wasn't holding her.

"Because if you think about it, you'll change your mind?"

She pulled away from him and took a step backward. Her body trembled with a combination of arousal and confusion. "Forget it," she said, feeling foolish and far too aggressive now that the mood had been broken.

"Is that your solution to everything? Forget it?" he asked. "Because I'm not forgetting. Any of this."

Shaking, she headed for the car, hoping she'd taken the right path, relieved when she heard his footsteps behind her.

She got in the passenger side and slammed the door.

Nick got in behind the steering wheel and started the engine.

He drove the entire way to Elmwood in silence. Ryanne didn't attempt to say anything, either, because she didn't know what to say. What could be said? The feelings tumbling inside her were a confusing mixture of embarrassment, hurt and anger. She'd never come so close to doing something so spontaneous and purely hormone driven, and the fact that Nick had been the one to reconsider—again—irked her no end.

Nick steered her car into the drive and carefully pulled into the garage, then switched off the engine. He removed the keys and held them out to her.

Ryanne took them and got out, automatically locking the car doors.

She headed for the house while Nick closed up the garage and fastened the padlock.

"Are you ever going to talk to me?" he called softly from behind her.

"I don't think so."

"What are you mad about?"

"I'm not mad."

"What then?"

"Never mind." She opened the back door.

He stepped right up behind her. "Are we on for the rest of the week?" he asked.

"That's probably not a good idea," she replied. She turned on the kitchen light and got a glass from the cupboard. From the pitcher in the refrigerator, she poured herself lemonade and drank it.

He was studying her, but she refused to meet his eyes. "If you want something, help yourself," she said.

Nick watched her guardedly. He wanted something, all right. He shouldn't have hesitated. Her frustration pleased him in a purely male way. "Not going to play anymore because you're mad at me?" he teased.

"Shut up, Nick."

"If I have a memory lapse, will you play with me again?"

She set her glass on the counter with a clank. "Shut up, Nick."

"Or what? You'll stop sharing your toys with me?"

"Or I'll wipe that smirk off your face."

"I'm shakin'," he replied.

She reached behind her and grabbed the glass, and before he had time to react, she tossed the remainder of the lemonade at him.

Chapter Eight

The cold liquid hit his chest. Not much had been left in the glass, but enough to soak through his shirt in a good-size blotch.

Her eyes widened with surprise at what she'd done. She studied him with growing trepidation on her flushed face.

"So that's how it's gonna be." He took three long strides, opened the freezer door and jimmied several ice cubes from the plastic bag where she'd stored them.

Ryanne squealed and ran out the back door before he turned around. He gave chase, the door slamming behind him. He studied the back of the house, listened and heard her footsteps moving around the side. The dark slowed him down, kept him from gaining on her, though he knew she was just ahead. His shoes pounded across the pavement of the front walk, then were muffled by grass again as he ran on. When she passed the dining room windows, the light from inside illuminated her perfectly, and he caught her playful, determined expression as she glanced over her shoulder.

The ice was freezing his fingers and had begun to drip through them.

Ryanne shot up the back steps, but he was right behind her. This was a game they'd played hundreds of times in the past. She would try to slam the door now and he'd push it open. The scenario played out just as he anticipated.

Once he got the door wedged open, she was shooting toward the dining room, those luscious legs revealed in the long side split of her filmy skirt. She would head straight for the front door to escape back outdoors.

Behind her, he slipped on a throw rug and hit his shoulder on a doorjamb before catching his balance and gaining on her. Always before when they'd played this game, she'd been taller, longer-legged, and had escaped. But this time his legs were the longer ones, and he caught up to her as she tried to yank open the front door.

Flattening a palm against the wood panel, he trapped her in the prison formed by his body.

Completely surprised, she spun around, her breath coming in pants, and flattened her back against the door.

Her eyes were wide, revealing her perplexity. A pulse beat at the base of her throat and her feminine scent rose up to envelope him in the hot humid foyer.

She lowered her gaze to his lips for a heated second. Every kiss and touch they'd shared still burned like liquid flame in his veins.

Nick raised the rapidly melting ice and ran it across her collarbone, watched as the cold stream dripped down her skin, the rivulet snaking beneath her little top. The moisture made dark spots on the fabric over her breasts. He brought the cubes up and ran them slowly over her jaw, along her cheek and across her lips.

"You suck at playing fair," she said to him, the anger missing from her tone now.

He lowered his head and kissed her cold wet lips. They warmed immediately, and she offered him her tongue. She tasted tart and sweet, like the lemonade she'd drunk, and he couldn't get enough of her. He couldn't deny his need for her anymore and he would trust her to know what she wanted.

Eagerly, she reached for him, and he pulled her close. They strained against each other, pressing, grasping, struggling for more closeness, more stimulating contact. Ryanne tugged at the hem of his T-shirt and he obliged her by yanking the damp fabric off over his head. Her delicate fingers on his chest were a touch so erotic, he groaned.

"You're sticky here," she said, and lowered her mouth to the spot where she'd splashed the lemonade. Her tongue darted out and tasted his skin. "Sweet, too."

He grasped the hem of her cotton top, and she raised her arms, letting him slip it off over her head. She untied a fabric sash, and her skirt slid down her thighs to pool on the floor at her feet.

Nick studied her pink-tipped ivory breasts, enjoyed the teasing sight of the tiny triangle of silk and lace she wore. He'd thought about her underwear in great detail ever since that night he'd barged into her room and seen her in nothing but. Bending on one knee, he reached for her sandals and pulled the straps from her heels. She kicked the shoes aside and placed her hands on his shoulders.

Finally he was able to see and touch the woman he'd desired for so long. He cupped her hips and pressed his cheek to her belly worshipfully.

The scent and softness of her skin were aphrodisiacs to his already acute senses. He pressed kisses across her stomach, up the valley between her breasts, took a nipple in his mouth and heard her sharp intake of breath.

While he dimly thought he should go slowly and enjoy every moment, Ryanne's incredible responsiveness urged him to proceed more quickly. Somehow they moved to the stairs, the aged wood creaking under his weight.

"Sit," she told him.

He obeyed and stared at her beauty while she removed his shoes and tossed his socks over the railing. She leaned forward to kiss him, and once again he was lost in her taste and warmth and sweet passion. He caressed her breasts the way she'd liked earlier, and she stepped up to straddle his lap.

He cupped her hips through the flimsy material and drew her flush against the straining erection just beneath a layer of denim.

"Upstairs," she said urgently against his mouth.

Somehow she disentangled herself and took his hand, leading him to her dark bedroom.

She switched a nightlight on, dimly revealing her form. Her hair was a wild tangle of honey-blond curls, her lips puffy from his kisses. Her skin glowed from the heat and dampness of the night air. She tossed a pile of ruffled pillows from the bed and pulled down the chenille spread.

At least it was a double, he thought, unbuckling his belt and watching her strip off the panties and wait for him on the pink-checked sheets.

She didn't look away as he removed his jeans and underwear in one fell swoop. Instead she smiled and reached for him. He stretched out beside her, taking her in his arms, shuddering at the silken slide of her ivory skin along his entire body.

"I can't believe this is you, Nick," she said, stroking his back and shoulders, bringing her hands around to enclose his swollen hardness and elicit a curse from him. "When did you get so...so..."

"Big?" he suggested with a grin.

"Sexy," she finished.

This was not how friends behaved. He knew it in the back of his sex-starved mind. She'd insisted that he remain her friend, and he would try, but everything had changed, and sooner or later she would have to face that. But not tonight. Not now. Ryanne had finally allowed Nick into a portion of her world, and he meant to enjoy it.

He pushed her back onto the pillows, leaned over her and touched her cheek tenderly. The kiss he gave her was meant to show her just how long he'd waited for this moment, how deeply he felt for her and how he would gladly accept however much or little she was willing to give him. Because he loved her. And he always had.

He deepened the kiss and she pressed herself against him, urged him to move over her. Touching her, he discovered she was slick and swollen with readiness, and he thought his heart would stop at the sheer ecstasy of her eagerness.

She was impatient, greedy, and he entered her swiftly, matching his strokes to her sounds of pleasure and her corresponding movements. The remaining pillows fell to the floor; the sheets tangled at their feet. Their bodies grew slick with perspiration.

Ryanne dug her nails into the small of his back and wordlessly demanded he not slow down. Her entire body tensed and then jerked, and she cried out. Nick's release was quick and fierce and left him shaky from exertion. He rolled to one side, taking her with him. Finding the eyelet-edged sheet, he used a bunched up wad to dry his forehead and then Ryanne's damp body.

They turned onto their backs, their breath labored, their skin cooling. Nick hazily registered the fact that a fan in the window had been blowing ineffectively across them the whole time.

"Nick?"

"What?"

"Was that normal?"

"It usually takes longer. It's been a while, and you've driven me crazy for a week."

She chuckled. "I didn't mean that. I meant, well…I don't know."

He rolled his head to look at her in the dim glow. "You think it was perverted or something?"

"No, no," she said, waving a hand limply. "I mean—is that the way it usually is?"

"The way what is?"

"You know."

"Sex?" he asked.

"Yeah."

"It certainly wasn't usual for me."

"Really?"

"Yeah."

"Didn't you and Holly have good sex?"

"We had sex. Never that intense."

"Oh."

A minute passed where she said nothing, and his mind kicked into overdrive. "What about you and Mason?"

"You remembered his name."

"Well…yeah."

"It was just sort of expected," she said. "Like we should do it because we were married. But nothing like this ever happened."

His heart had slowed to a normal cadence, and he concentrated on her words.

"We probably only did it ten times the whole time we were married," she added.

He propped himself on his elbow to look at her. *Ten times in how many years?* What was wrong with the man? "And you said Mason was the first?"

"He was."

"So…" Nick's mind rolled the information over, working to assimilate this surprising data. "You'd only had sex ten times before tonight?"

"About."

He laced his fingers through her hair and combed out tangles. "Something is definitely wrong with that man."

She turned to meet his eyes in the semidarkness. "Or with me."

He shook his head. "Sweetheart, there's not a thing wrong with any part of you." Just talking about it, lying here beside her and inhaling her scent, had him wanting her again. He pressed his erection against her thigh and her eyes widened. "In fact...what would you say to ten times in one night?"

"I really have to go," he said an hour or so later. Neither of them had looked at the clock. "I haven't checked on Jamie, and even though I switched on the intercom to Dad's room, I need to make sure everything's okay."

"We haven't reached ten yet."

"Are you trying to kill me?"

"It was your suggestion."

"That it was. Your skin is so soft right here...."

"Mm-hmm. Your hands feel so good on me, Nick. Sometimes I don't think I can stand it."

"Is this really happening, Rye?"

"I think so. Oh...oh, yes. You could check on Jamie and come back."

"What will you do while I'm gone?"

"Take a bath?"

"Don't do that."

"Why not?"

"Because we can take one together when I get back."

"I'll light candles."

"I'll hurry."

They didn't reach ten, but the following morning Ryanne's unaccustomed body knew they'd made a good start on the goal. She soaked in a tub of warm water, thinking about the slide of Nick's soap-slicked skin against hers as they'd nestled together in the big old cast-iron tub in the wee hours of the morning.

"I've kept you up all night," she'd said as they kissed with open mouths, their wet hair dripping on each other.

"You certainly have," he'd replied with a lecherous wiggle of his dark brows.

Ryanne smiled at the memory and stretched languorously in the water. She'd never known such physical intimacy was possible. Never understood the concept of crazy, head-over-heels physical or emotional attraction until this very moment, while her mind was clear and her body satiated and sore, yet still greedy for Nick Sinclair.

He was at his job now, but if he came into this room right this moment, she would once again be willing and eager for his lovemaking. Her desire for him frightened her, threatened her sense of independence. She'd never needed anyone, not ever. She'd set out to accomplish her scholastic and career goals, depending on no one but herself, and she would continue to do so.

Even after losing everything and being betrayed, she had pulled herself up and devised a plan to move forward and fix things. Her life was not going to play out here in Elmwood. She had a couple of good job prospects to consider, and in order to pay her debts, she would be taking one of them.

Nick would not be a part of her life.

Beneath the minimal weight of the sudsy water, her chest felt heavy at the realization. She closed her eyes and remembered every divine detail of their intimacy. She'd never imagined she would experience anything so raw, yet so beautiful...so humbling and yet so empowering. And never, never in a million years and a million fanciful dreams had she imagined Nick would be the man to awaken her to the sensual side of herself.

Nick believed she was going back to California. Perhaps to him, she was a brief diversion—a discreet means to satisfy a physical hunger. He'd told her that he didn't form relationships with women in town because of the gossip it would create, but she didn't want to believe she'd simply been handy. In her heart of hearts, she knew he desired her as deeply as she did him.

Could he show her such tenderness and pleasure and then simply say goodbye? It was his nature to give.

Maybe he gives too much. Maybe you don't give enough.

The voice of her conscience had her opening her eyes and facing reality. This new sensual discovery was too wonderful to deny herself just because it was temporary. She was too selfish to vow to go back to the way things had been before, even though that's what her moral sense told her she should do.

Ryanne pulled the stopper to let the water run down the drain, and stood to dry off. She studied her body in the mirror, really seeing it for the first time, appreciating her femininity with a whole new outlook.

She wanted this time with Nick. She needed it. She would just have to keep in mind that it would be over soon, and enjoy every brief minute while it lasted.

The sun beat down mercilessly as Nick chased another turkey across the road and into the tall dusty grass. Striding forward, he flushed half a dozen more out into the open and grabbed as many as he could. The one he'd been chasing ran down the highway to join a dozen more of the pathetically ugly creatures.

"Nobody can say this isn't a glamorous job," he told the driver of the overturned semi, who'd been taken to the clinic to be treated for a few cuts and bruises and then driven back to help round up the escaped poultry. At least a hundred wooden crates lay broken or open along the roadside, and all available deputies and manpower had been called out to help with the cleanup.

"I came around that turn back there, and smack-dab in the middle of the road were half a dozen cows," the driver explained yet again with exasperation.

Nick's deputy, Bryce Olson, hauled a crateful of the pale, sickly looking fowl to the back of a nearby pickup, then grimaced at the smears on his brown pant leg. He emitted a vivid curse before glaring at the semi driver and descending the bank once again with an empty crate.

"It's going to be tomorrow morning before they get out here to haul my rig up," the driver said.

"What are we going to do with all these turkeys

in the meantime?'' Nick asked. "They can't sit out here in the sun and fry.''

"I called the farm. They won't take 'em back,'' the harried man explained. Nick concentrated on the white bandage on the man's forehead and tried to remember this had been an accident.

"I'm trying to find someone to come get them, but nobody wants to touch this mess.''

"I can understand that.'' Nick wiped his forehead with the back of a hand and adjusted his hat.

"My guess is they're going to write this load off.''

"And where does that leave us?'' Nick looked around in disgust. "Let me make a few calls.'' He climbed into his cruiser, started the engine and cranked up the air-conditioning. On even less sleep than usual, he was functioning at low capacity today, not a good condition for a man with a loaded gun and a low opinion of live turkeys.

Down the highway, Duane Quinn chased a couple of the odorous creatures; loose feathers flew in the sunlight.

Taking a drink of sun-warmed coffee from his cup on the console, Nick picked up his cell phone and made a few calls.

By noon the driver had been informed that his guess was correct. Nobody wanted to deal with this, and the shipment was being written off. His freight company couldn't get anyone out to help clean up until the following day.

Nick put his plan into action, and nearby farmers and businessmen arrived to carry away crates of free turkeys. An assembly line was set up at the Cooper farm, and turkeys were killed and dressed until late that night.

Every citizen who had a freezer soon had it stocked full, as did as the merchants who owned commercial freezers—at the store, the café and the steak house.

Nick got home late that evening to discover Ryanne with Jamie. "Hi, guys."

"Hi, Dad!" Jamie ran to give his father a hug, but backed away, wrinkling his nose. "You stink."

"Where's Pop?" Nick asked Ryanne.

"Helping with the cleanup somewhere," she replied. "I told him I'd be glad to come stay with Jamie."

"Thanks."

"No problem. We had dinner a little while ago. I saved you some."

"As long as it's not turkey." He looked her over with new appreciation, hoping she hadn't had a change of mind or any regrets about the night before.

She blushed under his gaze, then wrinkled her nose. "Go take a shower," she suggested.

He did, a long one, standing under the spray and letting it pound out the weariness in his shoulders. Jamie sat on the vanity and watched him shave, asking questions, chattering about his own day.

Ryanne had served up a plate of spaghetti for him, with a green salad on the side, and she and Jamie played on the computer while he ate.

Nick put in a video for his son, and after about half an hour, tucked him into bed. When he returned to Ryanne in the family room, she was looking through a photo album.

Nick relaxed into the cushions of the comfortable

leather sofa and propped his crossed ankles on the trunk.

Ryanne wore a tender expression when she turned to him. "Some day, huh?"

"My life went from ecstasy to torment in a matter of hours."

"Ecstasy, you say."

"Pure."

She smiled and moved over to snuggle up beside him. Nick wrapped his arm around her shoulders and kissed her temple. With the album in her lap, she nestled her head on his shoulder and rested her palm over his heart. Nick picked up her hand and kissed her fingers.

They sat that way, comfortable, comforting, for a long, easy time. Finally, Ryanne shifted, sitting up and turning her attention back to the photographs.

"What are you looking at?"

"I found a stack of old albums, and I brought a few over to show Jamie. Here's us." She lifted the book and showed him a photograph of the three of them—Ryanne, Nick and Justin—playing on the beach at Lake Okoboji. In the shot beside it, they rode brightly painted horses on the old-fashioned carousel at the amusement park. "We went there several summers, didn't we?"

Nick nodded.

"My dad spent all his time near the cabins reading, but your dad took us fishing and boating."

Nick had avoided pictures of his younger brother, avoided the painful memories they dredged up. Ryanne turned to him, intuitively understanding. "This is painful for you?"

He nodded.

She closed the album and set it on the floor. "Maybe if you talked about it, about Justin, it would help."

"Like you talk about Mason?"

That shut her up, though Nick hadn't intended to be cruel. She meant well, but she hadn't shared much about her life while they'd been apart, and there were things he didn't want to talk about, either.

"Birdy called me today," Ryanne said, changing the subject.

"Yeah?"

"We're having lunch tomorrow." She nestled back into Nick's embrace. "It seems really weird seeing her after all this time."

"Seemed weird seeing me, too, didn't it?"

"That's because you *are* weird."

She'd made him smile, and he hugged her with appreciation for understanding his need for privacy. "Like Birdy's not." He nuzzled Ryanne's cheek, and she turned her face to his.

She ran her index finger over Nick's lower lip; he ducked his head to give her a quick kiss. She did it again, and this time when he kissed her, she wrapped her arm around his neck and hung on.

Being a woman with a will of iron and a fierce independent nature, she found that needing someone was foreign to her. Therefore Ryanne didn't understand this wild urgent *wanting* she felt for this man. How he instinctively knew the measures of delicacy and strength that wound her tighter and tighter, she couldn't fathom, but he proved it again with kisses that went from tender and seeking to forceful and possessive. Somehow he anticipated each degree of intimacy until she was delirious with the pleasure of his kisses and his stroking hands.

His mouth left hers and they breathed the same air, anticipation and eagerness making her breathless. "I can't leave tonight," he said. "My dad's not here." He kissed her, and just as acute disappointment threatened to wash over her, he suggested, "We can go up to my room."

She took his hand, and he turned off lights. She climbed the stairs ahead of him, Nick running his hands over her bottom. At the doorway, he kissed her. "I'll check on Jamie."

"I'm not going anywhere."

He moved down the hallway.

Ryanne stepped into Nick's darkened room. Not locating a switch on the wall, she made her way by the moonlight filtering in through the window, and turned on a bedside lamp.

No trophies lined the bureau or the shelves above it. The stuffed lizard and model cars were gone. The furniture was contemporary oak—a wide king-size bed, not too tidily made, and an open armoire revealing a TV and a stereo. A comfortable overstuffed chair sat near the window, with two stacks of books on the table beside it.

Ryanne picked up the one on top: *A Sleep Manual,* written by an M.D., Ph.D. The one beneath it was a mystery novel by a popular author. She spotted a *Blue Book* of auto prices, and another car book. On the other stack, the title *Mars and Venus in the Bedroom* leaped out at her. She flipped it open and noted that the receipt being used as a bookmark was only two days old. A smile inched up the corner of her lips. An ink pen and a tablet lay beneath the book, and her fingers itched to unearth it and see what was written.

The door closed softly behind her, and she turned to find Nick approaching.

Ryanne set down the book. "He's asleep?"

"The kid sleeps like a rock."

"You're an eclectic reader."

His gaze flickered to the stack of reading material and back to her. Nick reached for the lamp and plunged the room into darkness. "Look," he said, taking her hand and leading her to the window.

Through the open drapes, her mother's house was plainly visible. Ryanne could even see the window fan running in the dining room, though the house was dark. She'd left while it was still light.

"I can see right into your room when you have the light on and the curtains open," he confessed. He stepped close behind her and wrapped his arms around her.

Ryanne leaned back against his hard male strength. "At least you don't have a pair of binoculars or a telescope set up here." A minute later she added, "Do you?"

"No. But there's a Camcorder in the closest."

"With a telephoto lens, no doubt. Have you seen anything good lately?"

He chuckled. "Not lately. I got quite an eyeful when I was about fourteen, though."

She turned in his embrace. "You did?"

"Um-hmm."

"You never said anything."

"Like I was going to tell you I'd seen your boobs. Sometimes I wondered if you did it on purpose."

She pulled back and gaped at him. "Why would I do that?"

"To make me crazy."

She punched him in the arm. "You take that back. I'm not an exhibitionist!"

He captured her hand and laughed. "Yeah, well, I'm not a voyeur."

She allowed him to tug her back into his embrace, then she fitted her body along the length of his and looked up at him. He raised a hand to thread his fingers through her hair. "I want you, Rye. Are you okay with this?"

She appreciated the freedom to change her mind, but she wanted it as much as he did. She glanced toward the door.

"I locked it," he said.

She met his eyes. "I'm okay with it."

He kissed her, and she melted as she had before. He led her to the edge of his bed and urged her to sit. When she did, he slipped her sandals from her feet and rubbed one foot sensuously, then the other. Kneeling, he trailed his palms up her calves, sending a shudder through her already half-aroused body.

Ryanne touched his cheek, still in awe over this unexpected and thoroughly enticing new development, still shocked to find out she was more than okay with it. She was downright starved for it.

Chapter Nine

Leaning forward, Nick kissed both her knees, then one thigh. She had entirely too many clothes on, but she didn't want to rush him. He was doing just fine. And as if she'd thought it aloud, he reached for the buttons on her sleeveless summer shirt and unfastened them from top to bottom. He hooked a finger in the center of her bra between her breasts. "A bra this time."

"I usually wear one."

"But not on our drives."

She grinned and shrugged out of the shirt. "Not then."

"Is this one of those miracle bras? Because I don't think you need one."

"A miracle or a bra?"

He leaned forward and kissed the exposed flesh above the lacy cup. "Either one."

She bracketed his face and luxuriated in the sensation of his mouth on her skin. Ah, the pleasure this man gave her was pure rapture for a body and a heart that had never known the arousing possibilities. He made her feel. He made her come alive, become aware of herself in a way she'd never been.

Pulling away long enough to tug his shirt over his head, Nick returned to nuzzle her along the edge of her bra. Ryanne wondered if her touches felt as good to him, and knew they must when she caressed his muscled shoulders and elicited a soft groan. Feathering kisses up her neck, he cupped her breast and kneaded it through the lacy fabric. "Front or back?" he breathed under her ear.

"What?"

"The catch. Front or back?"

"Oh. Back."

He reached around and loosened the hooks, and Ryanne dropped the undergarment to the floor. His lips traveled an erotic course across her collarbone and over the crests of flesh, making her anticipate, making her hold her breath.

He guided her into the center of the bed, removing the rest of his clothing and joining her, only to sit on his knees and admire her in the shaft of moonlight. His broad shoulders and narrow waist and hips made a tantalizing silhouette in the shadows. He skimmed her thighs with silky strokes, raised a knee and kissed strategic spots along her ankle, calf and the inside of her thigh, then repeated the caresses on the other leg.

Gently turning her over, he continued the onslaught of inflaming kisses across her shoulders and down her spine, to the backs of her knees, the small of her back... She lost her breath and her sense of time and place here with him. She became a creature of acute senses, her skin tingling, her body warm and throbbing...aching for more of his touch.

"Nick," she said with a ragged sigh.

"What, Rye?"

"You're killing me."

Lying alongside her, he half covered her with his naked body and whispered into her ear, "What a way to go, eh?"

Pulling free of his weight, she turned impatiently to embrace him. She kissed him with fierce ardor, her need heightened to an intense peak by his inciting gentleness.

He cupped her through the silk of her panties; she gasped against his mouth, pressed urgently against his hand.

He made quick work of slipping them off, touched her again, intimately, knowledgeably, taking her mouth at the same time. Ryanne's entire body tensed and hummed with soaring pleasure. She gripped Nick's shoulder, pressed her feet into the mattress and plunged into ecstasy with all-pervasive shudders.

When she finally came back down to earth, Nick was kissing her neck, taking tiny nips of her earlobe and rubbing his palm in a circle over her abdomen.

Embarrassed over her complete abandonment to the feelings he created, she tucked her head down and curled her body.

Nick brushed her hair aside. "What's the matter?"

"What you must think of me," she said against his chest.

"I think you're the sexiest woman I've ever

known,'' he said without hesitation. ''I think you're beautiful and smart and passionate—even though you never knew it before—and it turns me on completely to give you pleasure.''

Ryanne raised her gaze to his, trying to see his eyes in the darkness, but reassured by the sincerity in his voice. She touched him, finding him hot and wanting. He coaxed her to move over him, sit astride and take him inside her.

It was her turn to test the limits of his endurance, take him nearly to release and then pause to let the tide pass. She didn't feel she had to match his energy now. Though the lovemaking was good, it was different, unhurried, and she indulged in the opportunity. Before, she'd experienced an increasing enjoyment as he took her to the top of a mountain. Now she was dancing on top of the world with him.

''If you want me to wait, slow down,'' he warned her, gripping her thighs.

She leaned forward so her breasts grazed his chest, but didn't slow.

Nick cupped her buttocks and helped her movements. She felt him pulse inside her, and she relaxed, resting her cheek against his shoulder. Beneath her breasts, his heart pounded, eventually slowing. Lazily, he caressed her back, her shoulder and neck…her cheek. His hands fell idle. His breathing evened out, deep and rhythmic, and Ryanne rested there for a long time, feeling safe and wanted.

Finally she moved to his side, and his hands fell loosely to the mattress. Tugging a sheet up over them both, she lay beside him, listening to him breathe. Minutes later, she, too, slept.

* * *

Dawn crept through the drapes Nick had never gotten around to closing the night before, turning the inside of his eyelids a rosy hue. Without opening his eyes, he sensed the difference in the room—in his bed. Snuggled along his side was a silky warm, feminine body. The scent of musk and woman was overpowering his senses. Thinking back to his last memory, a jolt of surprise brought him to wakefulness.

He'd fallen asleep.

Nick opened his eyes, almost disoriented in his own bedroom. He remembered nothing of trying to fall asleep, no thoughts, no relaxation practices. The last thing he remembered was ultimate satisfaction and the joy of being with Ryanne.

She slept on her side, facing him in an endearing tangle of sheets and smooth bare limbs, her honey-blond hair a riot of waves across the pillow and one side of her face. God, she was beautiful. Her golden-dark lashes rested against creamy, fair skin, and her lips were pink and deliciously puffy. One pink nipple peeked out above the hem of his forest-green sheet.

He'd fallen asleep!

Nick tried to remember what time it had been. Not later than eleven—twelve at the very latest. He couldn't remember the last time he'd slept that many hours in a row, and he'd never awakened feeling so rested and at peace. And they'd made love only once.

He glanced at the clock in the predawn light. It would be at least another hour or so before his dad or Jamie roused.

Without disturbing Ryanne, he used the bathroom; she was still sleeping when he returned. He kissed her shoulder, inhaling her scent, branding it on his brain so he'd never forget when she was gone. Burying his nose in her hair, he let the smell and the memory of the night before arouse him.

She stirred and opened her eyes. Recognition swept over her and her cheeks tinged a rosy pink. A woman who blushed. He took her hand and kissed her fingers.

"Sorry I fell asleep on you."

"You weren't on me." She grinned.

"You know what I mean."

"You were beat. I kept you up late the night before."

"You didn't do so bad at keeping me up last night, either."

"Awake. I meant awake."

"In fact, I'm up now."

"Already?"

"Already."

"But I should go before your family wakes up."

"We have time."

"Oh, my. Did you learn these things from that book?"

"Which book?"

"You know which book. Oh, my-y."

They would have had time for her to get away if Nick hadn't found more inventive ways to keep her in his bed. As it was, when Jamie knocked, Nick had to hurry out and close both him and his son in Jamie's room long enough for Ryanne to tiptoe down the stairs.

"Coffee's on!" Mel called from the kitchen.

Guiltily, as though she was a teenager caught in the

act, she slipped out the front door and darted across the side yard.

Forty-five minutes later, she was sitting at the kitchen table in her lightweight robe, her hair drying, when Nick stepped off his back deck and unlocked the door of the cruiser parked alongside the garage.

Ryanne carried her cup of coffee to the front porch and returned his wave as he pulled into the street and drove past.' That simple little encounter made her heart flutter as though she were a foolish schoolgirl with her first crush. Each day and every meeting with Nick was more dangerous than the last. She was in serious peril of losing her iron control and doing something stupid. Like getting emotionally involved.

She didn't need any more complications, and he was definitely turning into a complication. Maybe it was time to pull back, cut her losses before anyone found out. This morning had been a close call. If Mel or Jamie knew, she would feel obligated to make some sort of commitment, for propriety's sake, and she couldn't do that. Neither did she want Jamie to get any mistaken hopes about her being a permanent part of his life.

Struggling with the conflicting feelings of what she should do and what she wanted to do, Ryanne tidied her bedroom and the kitchen, dressed for lunch, and was just preparing to leave when the doorbell rang.

"Morning, Mrs. Davidson," Pat, the mailman, greeted her. "Registered letter today."

Ryanne glanced at the envelope, recognizing the return address. She met the man's eyes. "Thanks."

He handed over the green-and-white slip for her to sign. Would he think it odd that she had to sign for her mail from the IRS? A lot of people got quarterly statements, but they didn't have to sign for them. He handed her the envelope, as well as the rest of her mail, and all she could think of was that her secret was slipping out. Maybe she was making too much of it; he probably saw registered mail all the time, and as a professional, he wouldn't discuss her mail with others.

Pat gave her a little wave and headed for the Sinclair house.

Ryanne read the notification of her delinquent balance, her heart sinking. Another letter, from her attorney, informed her that her retainer had run out and if she wanted any further legal advice or assistance, she would have to make payments.

Ryanne placed the letters neatly on the dining room table, took a deep breath and resolved to make a dreaded stop on the way to meet Birdy. She had no choices left. She would have to sell the one thing that would hurt the most—her car.

When she pulled up in front of the Steak House, Birdy was waiting near the entrance. "Hey, Ryanne!"

"Hey, Birdy."

"I heard talk around town that you had a fancy red sports car. What's up with this one?"

Ryanne glanced at the plain little, used sedan, a sick feeling in the pit of her stomach. The Viper represented all of her dreams, her accomplishments, but they were just so much dust now. She drew a deep breath and willed herself to get over it. "My car's on Forrest Perry's lot. This one's a loaner until mine sells."

"Not sure what you want?"

"Something like that."

"Well, let's go get a seat in the front, where we can see everyone who comes in."

Ryanne followed her, and Elizabeth Monroe ushered them to a booth. The place was clean and brightly lit by the sunshine pouring through the open shutters on the enormous windows. Ryanne remembered the place as dark and outdated, but apparently the Monroes had remodeled sometime during their ownership.

"This is Valerie," Birdy said, indicating the fresh-faced teenager who had come to take their drink orders. "She and her brother, Lance, help their folks run this place."

"Hi," Valerie said. "You're Sheriff Sinclair's neighbor, right?"

"For the time being."

"Ryanne and I went to school together," Birdy said.

"I can't wait to get out of this town," Valerie told her. "I can't believe you'd want to take a vacation somewhere so *boring*."

"Well, when you need a rest, boring is good," Ryanne replied.

"Yeah, I guess."

Valerie took their orders and then went to fetch their drinks.

"So how have you been?" Birdy asked. "Besides ditching the old ball and chain, I mean."

"Fine, fine." Ryanne glanced over at two middle-aged women at a booth across from them. Their interest wasn't disguised. She smiled uncomfortably, and they smiled back, as though tickled at her recognition.

"I'll bet you meet a lot of glamorous people at your job," Birdy said. "What's it like, being a big shot at an advertising agency?"

Ryanne thought about the question for a moment. "Stressful. Everyone's in a hurry. Everyone's eager to launch a new campaign, get a jump on the season, be ahead of their competitors. There's a lot of game playing and good old boy practices, and there's always pressure to be the best to stay on top."

Birdy obviously hadn't been expecting that answer. She sat back in her seat. "Oh."

Ryanne hadn't really expected to give her that answer, either. Where had it come from? How long had she felt that way? At some point along the way, her career had stopped being the be-all and end-all of everything she'd ever wanted and believed in, and she hadn't taken time to consider her thoughts and feelings.

"But you like it?" Birdy asked.

Ryanne studied Birdy's upswept curly hair and her dangling, gold hoop earrings. "I like what it should be. What it could be. What I thought it was going to be when I got into it. I love the challenge of coming up with just the right marketing strategy, putting together the artists and the clients that will make it happen. I liked being my own boss."

"What about your friends? Or prospective relationships?"

Valerie served their iced tea and Ryanne squeezed her lemon slice into the glass. "I usually worked six or seven days a week. I didn't have a lot of time for much else.''

"You talk like it's in the past," Birdy said.

Ryanne ran a finger down the condensation on her glass and glanced up as the door opened and a couple in their twenties entered the restaurant and nodded at Ryanne and Birdy.

Her one tiny solitary consolation was that no one knew about what Mason had done. Her shame and embarrassment was still her secret—as long as the mailman didn't pass along any rumors. "I'm making a lot of changes," she said finally. "So a lot of that is in the past."

"Well, that's good. You need to have time to enjoy life. Take a detour out of the rat race and have some fun.''

"Yes." Ryanne gave Birdy a smile. Her old friend seemed genuinely interested in her life, not just in the latest gossip, and Ryanne found the knowledge comforting. "What about you? What's happening in your life? Any new prospects?''

"You've been in Elmwood for a while," Birdy replied with a derisive twist of her lips. "Have you seen anyone who looks like a prospect?''

Ryanne shrugged. "No single men?''

"Well, sure, a few. Dr. Kline. Garreth is his name. He's about our age, early thirties. Then there's Jon, who owns the construction company. Works all the time. George Kingsley runs the auto repair shop.'' She wrinkled her nose. "Dirty nails. A few guys from the plant. Nick, of course.''

Ryanne's heart leaped at the mention of Nick's name. "Have you dated any of them?''

"Jon and I used to date. I've gone to the movies and the casinos with a couple of the fellows from the plant."

"What about this doctor fellow?"

"I don't think I'm his type."

"How can you tell?"

"Probably the fact that he has a medical degree and I flunked out of beauty college."

Ryanne laughed. "Come on, give yourself more credit. You're smart and fun and you're still the prettiest girl in just about any room."

Birdy blushed and gave Ryanne an odd look. "Thank you, Rye. But if I was the prettiest in the room, you would have to be elsewhere."

Ryanne laughed. "Okay, thanks," she said. "Any other men?"

"Oh, sure. Nick and I have hung out some. But it's not like that."

"Like what?"

"No romantic involvement. He's wrapped up with the kid and his dad. I think after he was burned—by Holly, you know—he wasn't willing to let anyone else get too close. Besides, he keeps himself so busy taking care of everybody else, I've never known him to do things just for himself."

Ryanne had noticed that about Nick, too. Compared to him, she was the most selfish person she knew. But then, their lives had been different. She'd never had brothers or sisters to look after. Her mom was healthy, and had never needed her like Nick's mom had needed him.

They were in the middle of delicious chicken salad sandwiches when a loud siren interrupted. The restaurant grew silent and several people got up to go to the door.

"What's that?" Ryanne asked.

"The fire signal!" Birdy stood. "Let's go."

They crowded out onto the front walk as a clanging fire truck streaked past, the volunteer firemen, dressed in their gear, clinging to the running boards.

Curious townspeople poured out of buildings and houses, and Birdy and Ryanne melded into the crowd running toward where a black chimney of smoke belched into the summer sky.

"Where is it?" Ryanne asked.

"Pine Street," voices called from ahead.

They turned a corner, and through the crowd, the burning building, a low structure with a steel fence, came into view.

"The day care!" someone shouted.

A couple of women screamed and ran faster.

Ryanne's heart lurched in her chest at the sound of panic, and the words jelled in her mind. *The day care? Jamie!*

Chapter Ten

"Get back before I turn this hose on ya!" a fireman with a gray handlebar mustache, and dressed in a bright yellow coat, hollered at the approaching on-lookers.

On the opposite side of the street stood a gathering of women and children—babies crying, the older charges watching the proceedings in alarmed fascination. Ryanne immediately spotted Jamie, pushed through the crowd and ran forward.

He saw her coming and burst into tears.

"It's all right," she said, kneeling and hugging him close. His slender body trembled from the scare.

Ryanne glanced up at the dark-haired woman who held two babies, one howling and one sound asleep. Beside her was a crib on wheels, which held three more crying babies. "Can I help?" Ryanne asked.

"If you could take this one," she said. "My arm's going to sleep, and these other poor little guys got the ride of their lives coming across the street."

Ryanne disentangled herself from Jamie, stood and reached for the sleeping baby, then took her two charges back a few steps into the shade of a leafy maple tree in someone's yard, and sat down. Birdy came to sit beside her with another baby, and they watched the firemen chop a hole in the roof of the day care building.

The dark-haired woman, whom Jamie told Ryanne was Miss Lottie, relayed over and over again to spectators the terrifying experience of discovering the fire and getting all the children to safety.

Eventually all the little ones were quieted and, one by one, horrified parents who had heard the news came running for their kids.

Another siren sounded, and a patrol car parted the sea of observers. The car door opened and Nick sprang from the vehicle, his face a stony mask as he surveyed the bystanders.

Someone pointed him toward the yard where they waited, and he sprinted across the grass, relief crossing his features.

"Daddy!" Jamie shot up and met his dad on the lawn. Nick enveloped his son and hugged him soundly, then carried him back to where Ryanne and Birdy sat.

Lottie and Kris Benson, the day care providers, spoke to Nick for a moment. After some comforting words, he settled Jamie back beside Ryanne. "I have to move the people back so the firemen can do their job," he told his son. "You stay here with Rye, okay?"

Jamie nodded. "Okay, Dad."

Nick's eyes met hers and he gave her a brief nod, a sort of personal assurance, before turning away and doing his job. She could only imagine the fear that had struck his heart when he'd received a radio message about the emergency. He probably wanted nothing more at this moment than to sit and hug his boy, but as always, Nick was doing his duty. Taking care of others.

"We didn't pay for our lunch," Birdy said from beside her.

Ryanne glanced over at her and laughed.

"You know I wouldn't ask if I didn't have to," Nick said that night, as the three adults sat around the table in his kitchen. Mel had made them iced tea after a late supper. "But there won't be a facility for a few days, at least until Lottie can figure something out. The school has offered her a few rooms until the day care is rebuilt, but to open will take replacing cribs and toys and supplies that were lost today."

"The church would be more economical to cool," Mel said.

"Well, they'll have to work that out. But for a few days, I need help with Jamie. I don't expect you to do it all, Dad."

"Nick." Ryanne placed her fingers over Nick's on the table. "I'm glad to help."

"I know this is your vacation," he said to her, regret tingeing his tone. He turned his hand over and held hers. Ryanne considered the strength in his hands, compared it to the glimpse of vulnerability she'd seen on his face that afternoon when he'd scanned the crowd for his son. She looked into his eyes for a moment, a silent communication of trust, then became aware of their contact and drew away.

If Mel noticed anything, he gave no indication. Either he considered their touch a sign of friendship, or he suspected it was more and was leaving them their privacy. When he stood and said, "I think I'll catch the news in my room," Ryanne thought it was the latter.

"Night," they chorused.

He set his glass in the sink and disappeared down the hall.

"The humidity's dropped," Nick said. "Would you like to sit on the back deck for a while?"

"Sure."

He led her out to the cushioned glider and pulled her down beside him. He'd had the scare of a lifetime that afternoon when the dispatcher had radioed him about the fire. He'd been several miles outside of town when the call had come, and even though a second call had come through to assure him all the children were safe, he'd had to see Jamie for himself before the knot of terror in his chest had loosened.

He'd witnessed his father getting a call about his son, but Nick had never understood until now just how his dad must have felt the night Justin died. As careful as Nick was, as many ways as he tried to protect his family, some things just happened that were out of his control, and that frightened him.

"Jamie and I will do fine for a few days," Ryanne assured him.

"It would be easier on Dad if you stayed here," he said.

She glanced at him.

"You can put your things in the extra bedroom. For appearances."

"Whatever works best for you," she replied.

"I think it'll be easier for you in the long run, too," he said. "His clothes and toys and videos are here. There's plenty of his favorite foods."

"Okay, I'm sold. Besides, I like your air-conditioning."

"I feel like I'm pushing you. I wouldn't have asked if this hadn't happened."

It was a convenient way to spend their evenings together—and probably their nights—more inconspicuously, but he didn't want her to feel pressured into anything—not into watching Jamie, and definitely not into staying with Nick himself.

Last night's lovemaking had been phenomenal, and the sleep had been damned near as good. He hated to appreciate that this near disaster was a means of prolonging his time with her.

"Don't say another word and don't apologize," Ryanne said. "I'll stay with Jamie because I want to. Because it's something I can do for you." She leaned into him and placed her hand on his chest. "I want to. Will you just relax and let somebody do something for you for a change?"

"Okay."

They listened to the ordinary, reassuring night sounds, rocked, and Ryanne snuggled close. He loved having her here.

"I'm not used to having someone," he said, thinking aloud. "To pick up the slack with Jamie, I mean. Dad is great, but he needs his own time and he needs his rest."

"I can't imagine what it's like raising a child on your own," she said. "I know there are a lot of single parents, but that doesn't mean it's easy figuring out child care and handling emergencies and the like."

Nick smoothed his fingers over the warm, silky skin of her arm. "That's not when I miss having someone the most," he said.

"No? When?"

He thought a minute. "Good times, I'd have to say. Like every year when we have his picture taken. He's so damned good-looking with a fresh haircut and new clothes. I look at him and it just hurts sometimes. He smiles for the photographer, and I choose his poses from a package. And I think all the while, I should have someone to share this with—he should have a mom who looks at him and thinks he's the most handsome thing in the world, like I do."

Beside him, Ryanne was silent.

He rubbed her arm. "And I look back at all the pictures over all the years...pictures of him as a chubby little baby...pictures of him with his teeth missing, like this year...and I think there's somebody missing in all this."

"He showed me pictures of him and Holly."

"I don't care a damn about Holly leaving me, about her not being happy with me," he said. "It's Jamie she should have cared about. If I live to be a hundred, I'll never understand how she could walk away and never look back."

"Maybe she believed it was the best for Jamie."

Nick wanted to accept that. "Maybe."

"She knew that with you he'd be loved and well cared for."

"That doesn't make it right."

"Life sucks, Nick," she said softly. "And that's never right."

Nick had never said these things to anybody—not even in counseling, when he'd sought help for his insomnia. Sharing them with Ryanne seemed to fit into the right order of things.

He tilted her face up and kissed her pliant lips, losing himself in her warmth and comfort. She kissed him back, touching his jaw and chin with feathery strokes and placing her palm alongside his face. His body responded immediately to her caresses and the taste of her moist, responsive kisses.

"I should go get a few things," she said.

"Hurry."

"I will. Wait right here. Don't move."

Nick watched her cross the side lot, saw the lights come on in the house and go out minutes later. Not only was he grateful for her help, he was pleased at the events that had her coming to stay with him, however briefly. Eventually, she reappeared in the dark, a bag in hand.

"You waited," she said.

"Good things are worth waiting for."

"Read that on a card somewhere?"

"I think it was a poster in human growth and development class. Did you miss that one?"

She took his hand and urged him to stand, leaning her body into his. "Really want to wait?"

"Nope." He followed her into the house.

* * *

By midnight Ryanne was sleeping soundly, and Nick lay with her head on his shoulder, his body sated, his mind in overdrive. As usual. He didn't want to disturb her by getting up and turning on the television or going out to the garage to work for a couple of hours. Maybe this hadn't been such a bright idea.

He was just about to slip his arm out from under her when his cell phone rang. She jumped and sat up, clutching the sheet to her breasts.

Nick reached toward the night stand and grabbed his phone. "Sinclair."

"Nick. It's the Vincents." It was Duane Quinn's voice.

"Did Ann Marie call in?"

"Not this time. This time the kid called."

"Damn!" Nick stood and grabbed his boxers from the floor. He sat on the edge of the bed to pull them on with one hand, then stood to finish the task.

Ryanne turned on the light and blinked up at him.

"How long ago?" Nick asked.

"Just now. I called you, 'cause I know you can handle Eddie. Unless you want me to get this one."

"No, no, I'll go. What the hell's he doing at home, anyway? Shouldn't he be working?"

"Everybody gets a night off. Over."

Nick switched off the phone and grabbed a pair of uniform pants from a hanger.

"What is it?" Ryanne asked.

"I have to take a call," he replied. "Sorry the phone woke you."

"No…that's all right."

He jammed his shirttail into his pants, zipped them up and buckled on his automatic.

"Is this a dangerous call, Nick?" she asked with a frown.

"Not for me," he replied. Ann Marie was the one in danger, but everything he said to the woman fell on deaf ears. "I'll call if it's going to take very long."

"Okay." She stood and padded over to him. "What a way to wake up, huh?"

"Yeah." He kissed her, flipped the lock and backed out of the room, closing the door.

Thank goodness for Ryanne; he wouldn't have to wake his dad and let him know he was leaving. Backing out the cruiser, he headed for the Vincent place, dreading what he would find.

The trip seemed to take forever in the dark. He had to go slower and search for landmarks, but finally he reached the gravel drive. The house was dark, with a solitary yellow bug bulb piercing the night from beside the front door. He'd always made these calls in the morning in the past, so a late visit seemed out of the ordinary—if one could ever say domestic abuse calls were ordinary.

Nick approached the door, his straining ears hearing nothing, not even yelling or crying. The door was closed and locked when he tried the knob. He didn't like it. He knocked firmly. "Ann Marie? Eddie?"

A minute later, the door opened. A hollow-eyed boy stared out at him, sought to look around him into the darkness. "Sheriff Sinclair?"

"Dylan, where's your mom?"

"In the bathroom. I locked us in there."

Dylan moved aside and Nick dashed past. Behind

him, the boy closed and relocked the door. "Is your dad here?" Nick asked, still moving.

"He left. I locked us in the bathroom and he went away."

With the aid of a dim night-light, Nick found the bathroom. Ann Marie's darkened form slumped against the wall near the tub. Nick groped on the wall for a switch.

"It's here." Dylan tugged a string and a light came on, revealing his mother in the harsh glare. Blood ran from a gash on her forehead, and she cradled her left arm against her midriff.

The sight turned Nick's stomach. Not quite his worst fear at coming here, but close to it. She was alive, and he released a breath. He plucked his phone from his belt and hit a speed dial number. "Duane. Send a paramedic."

"Is it bad?"

"She's conscious. The boy's here. Stat." He hung up and knelt down beside the woman. "Dylan, do you have any ice in the freezer?"

"I think so."

"Why don't you bring some in a plastic bag or a dish towel or something?"

"Okay."

Nick reached up and grabbed a worn towel from a hook, ran cold water over it and held it to Ann Marie's forehead.

She cried softly, turning dark pleading eyes to him. "I know what you're going to say," she sobbed.

"No, you don't."

"You're going to say you told me so."

"No, I'm not. I'm going to say it's your responsibility to keep your son safe from this, and you haven't done that. How much has he seen? How much are you going to make him see? You want him to grow up thinking this is normal?''

She tried to shake her head, but Nick forced her to hold it still, while he wiped away blood. ''No. No, of course not,'' she said. ''I know, and I'm sorry. I just thought…I never thought Eddie'd go this far… especially not in front of Dylan. He loves his son.''

''You are the one who has to protect your son. And yourself. What would happen to Dylan if Eddie killed you?''

Her eyes opened wide in shock. Nick's words were meant to startle her into thinking, but he regretted hurting her. She grabbed his arm and lowered her head as she sobbed. ''Nick. Nick, will you help me?''

''I'll help you,'' he replied, anger and compassion warring inside. ''You make the decision, and I'll help you. Do you have any idea where Eddie has gone?''

She shook her head.

Dylan returned with a bread bag filled with ice cubes. Nick took the bag, wrapped another towel around it and placed it against Ann Marie's arm. She cried out in pain, then bit her lip.

''I think her arm's broke,'' the boy said to Nick.

Nick looked at the arm and back at Dylan. ''I think you're right. The ice will keep the swelling down so they can set it.''

Ann Marie studied her son with a ravaged expression in her eyes. ''Dylan?''

''Yes, Ma?''

''We're not going to stay here anymore. Your father needs help, and until he gets it, we're going away.''

At her words, Nick felt as though a band that had been constricting his chest broke loose.

Dylan's eyes were wide with uncertainty. ''Where will we go?''

''I don't know right now. But we'll be fine together, you and me.''

''For tonight, you can come to my house,'' Nick told him. ''While your mom's getting fixed up at the clinic.''

Tears glistened in the boy's eyes. ''Okay.''

Flashing lights and a short siren burst alerted them to the paramedics' van outside. ''Go open the door, Dylan,'' Nick said.

Dylan ran to obey.

''I'm holding you to this decision,'' Nick said to her.

''You know I'm serious,'' she replied. ''I've never said it before, but I'm saying it now. And I mean it.''

''I'm proud of you, Ann Marie.''

Two paramedics ran down the hall, a man and a woman. ''Her left arm is broken,'' Nick told them. ''The boy's coming with me.''

He phoned Duane again. ''I'm taking Dylan Vincent to my place. Forward calls to Sharon's and come out here and look for Eddie. I'll join you after I get the kid settled.''

Nick helped Dylan pack a change of clothing, then got him settled in the cruiser.

''I'm glad school's out for the summer,'' Dylan said. ''I'd hate to be in school tomorrow when everybody finds out we're leavin' my dad.''

"Understand it's for the best," Nick told him. "Your dad will have to get help in order to have his family back."

"I know."

At the house, Nick opened the sofa bed in the family room. While he was making it up, Ryanne came down the stairs in a shiny robe.

"This is Dylan," he told her. "He's spending the night."

"Hi, Dylan."

"Dylan, this is Mrs. Davidson. She's taking care of Jamie for me. She'll be upstairs if you need anything."

Ryanne offered Dylan something to eat and drink, then slipped back upstairs while Nick showed him the bathroom. Nick stood by while the boy climbed wearily into the bed. Even though he was several years older than Jamie, he seemed to need more reassurance. Not surprising, considering the things he'd seen in his home.

"Everything's going to be okay," Nick told him.

"Thanks, Sheriff."

"Nick," he said softly. "Just call me Nick."

Ryanne was sitting in the easy chair beside the light when Nick entered the room. "Couldn't sleep?" he asked.

"Strange room. You weren't here." She set down a book.

Nick explained about Dylan, and her eyes filled with compassion.

"Sorry to saddle you with another kid," he said.

"Don't apologize," she replied. "Thank you for trusting me to help."

"I have to leave again, try to find the boy's dad. Get some sleep."

"What about you? You'll be exhausted."

He leaned over her and kissed her. "I'll go in late in the morning."

She touched his face. "You're a good man, Nick Sinclair."

"Just doing my job."

"I don't think so."

He kissed her again and left.

After a few awkward moments the following morning, Jaime and Dylan became fast friends, and Ryanne didn't see them except when they were hungry or thirsty. Nick slept on and off until ten, woke with a headache and ate the breakfast Ryanne prepared for him.

"Where's dad?" Nick asked.

"In the garden while there's some shade this morning," she told him. "He promised me zucchini bread this afternoon."

Nick nodded and took a sip of his coffee to swallow an aspirin.

"Did you find the boy's father last night? I was asleep when you came in."

"Yes. He's in jail. Ann Marie's going to press charges. And then she'll be finding a place to stay." Nick explained the ongoing situation and his frustration at not being able to do anything to help until Ann Marie was ready to make a change. "I kept thinking I was going to drive out there someday and find her dead. Eddie's one mean drunk."

"Thank goodness she finally made the right choice," Ryanne said.

The back door burst open and Jamie led Dylan into the kitchen.

"Whoa," Nick called out.

"We need more plastic bags, Dad!"

Dylan's greeting was a little more subdued. "Morning, Sheriff Sin—I mean—Nick."

"Good morning, boys. What do you need the bags for?"

"Grampa is filling bags with zucchini. Me 'n' Dylan put them on people's doorknobs, then ring the bell and run. It's fun."

Ryanne's eyes showed her puzzlement, but Nick knew exactly the trick his dad was employing. He took a stash of plastic grocery bags from a cupboard and handed them to his son. "Zucchini multiplies like rabbits," he told Ryanne with a grin. "You have to get rid of them somehow."

Jamie ran to Ryanne. "Will you come open your garage and show Dylan the Viper? Please?"

Nick was about to suggest that they wait awhile when Ryanne replied, "Well, actually, Jamie, the Viper's not in my garage."

"It ain't? Where is it?"

Nick didn't even correct his grammar; like his son, he simply waited expectantly for a reply.

"It's, um, it's over at Heartland Auto Deals. On the lot."

"What's it over there for?" Jamie asked, echoing Nick's thoughts.

"I'm selling it."

Chapter Eleven

"**Y**ou're *selling* it?" Nick asked, disbelief in his voice.

"Why're ya sellin' it?" Jamie asked at the same time.

Ryanne busied herself with placing plates in the dishwasher. "I didn't really need such a fast car. I got to thinking it was probably a little too flashy."

"But you loved that car," Nick said.

"Loved is a little strong," she denied. "It's just a car. No big deal. I'll get another one."

Her easy dismissal had a ring of untruth that disturbed Nick. "What are you driving now?"

"Forrest gave me a loaner so the Viper could sit in his showroom."

"How do you expect to sell a car like that in Elmwood?" he asked.

"He's advertising it through the dealership. It'll get exposure."

"You never said anything...." Nick let his words trail off and he gave a lame shrug.

"I didn't need to say anything, did I?" She seemed irritated with his comments. "It's my car, isn't it?"

Uncomfortable with the turn of conversation, Nick stood and carried his cup to the sink. "Sure. Sorry."

"It's just...not a big deal."

"Okay." He turned aside. "You boys behave yourselves. Dylan, I might bring your mom back here this afternoon. I called and she's checked out of the clinic, but she has some business to take care of."

"Where's my dad?"

Nick glanced at Jamie.

"It's okay," Dylan said perceptively. "I told him."

"Your dad's in jail. He'll have to put up bond money to get out before his trial. Your mom's pressing charges this time."

"That's good, isn't it?"

"It's very good. It means the court will make your dad get the help he needs."

Dylan nodded, and he and Jamie ran back outdoors.

Nick grabbed his hat from the counter. "I'll see you tonight."

Ryanne stepped close to lift her face for his kiss. "Don't worry. We'll be just fine."

Nick kissed her, studied her lovely features for a moment, thinking he didn't really know her, then turned to leave. The whole bit about selling the car just didn't make sense. He knew she loved that car, and no amount of denial on her part made him think she didn't. Something wasn't right, but he sure couldn't put his finger on it. If he didn't know better…if she wasn't a big shot West Coast advertising exec, he'd think she was strapped for cash.

Nick buckled himself into the cruiser, cranked up the air-conditioning and headed for the station. Anyone who didn't run air in this heat, especially when they were used to a dryer climate…

Pictures of the boxes he'd seen in the Whitaker dining room that first night when he'd let himself into the house and surprised Ryanne flashed through his mind—jewelry cases, odds and ends, books and computer software. She'd brought her computer along. Her stereo. How many people took a stereo on vacation, unless it was a portable one?

It had seemed then as if she'd brought enough with her to move in, but why would she be moving into her mother's house when she'd always hated Elmwood? Maybe she was more devastated about her divorce than she'd let on. But that didn't stack up—not with the way she had connected with Nick, the way she made love to him. Maybe he was just a rebound fling, but that didn't seem right, either. At least he didn't want to think so.

He'd always felt that Ryanne was holding something back, and that was her prerogative. They hadn't made any promises, no commitments. They both knew her time here was temporary. Her business was her own.

But he certainly couldn't help being curious.

When Nick brought Ann Marie Vincent to the house that afternoon, Ryanne hardly recognized her as the vibrant girl who'd been a year or so behind her in school. Of course, the bruised and swollen face distorted her appearance, but her body language spoke volumes. Maybe it was pain; her arm was in a cast. Who knew what other unseen injuries she'd suffered? But it was the way she didn't quite meet Ryanne's eyes that made the difference.

"I heard you were in Elmwood," Ann Marie said after Nick left for the station. "News travels fast around here."

Ryanne nodded. She offered Ann Marie a seat in the family room and brought a cushion for her arm to rest on. The fingers that protruded from the end of the cast were purplish and swollen. "Don't I know it."

"I suppose I'm the talk of the town today." Nervously, Ann Marie pushed her dark bangs away from her forehead.

Ryanne couldn't deny her words. She certainly felt like the object of gossip often enough herself, and she knew how unsettling it was.

A few minutes later the boys burst into the house, their faces damp and flushed from exertion.

"It's really hot out there," Jamie gasped, flopping on the carpet and spreading his arms.

Dylan sat at his mom's feet. She gave him a smile.

"Why don't you boys stay in and cool off for a while?" Ryanne suggested. "How about a video and some lemonade?"

"Popcorn?" Jamie asked.

"What's a video without popcorn?"

While the boys watched their show, the women got reacquainted. Sometimes, when she laughed, Ann

Marie seemed like the person Ryanne had known briefly so long ago. She wondered if she herself had changed as much, and if any of the changes had been for the better.

Nick arrived home, and they ate supper in the dining room—burgers and fried zucchini, along with sliced tomatoes and fresh corn. The boys ate corn on the cob until Nick swore it was coming out their ears.

Nick took Ryanne aside later, pulling her down the hall.

She wrapped her arms around his neck. "Been dying to kiss me?"

He kissed her. "Of course. But I have something to ask you."

"What is it?"

"I want to ask Ann Marie to stay here for a few days—just until she gets on her feet, and gets used to the cast and the pain eases up. We have an extra bedroom, but I know the load of the extra work will fall to you, so I—"

"Of course. Ask her to stay."

"You're sure you won't mind?"

"Not at all."

"Thanks, Rye." He kissed her again.

For the next three days, things went as smoothly as possible with two rowdy boys who got bored and then amused themselves in new and inventive ways. On the third evening, they had finished dinner and with one arm Ann Marie was helping Ryanne carry dishes to the sink when the phone rang.

Mel answered it on the second ring. "Evelyn! How are you?"

Ryanne's attention riveted on his voice. Why was her mother calling?

"Oh," he said, his voice gone serious. "Oh, my. Yes, dear. Yes, of course, here she is." He held the phone out. "Ryanne, it's your mother."

She took the phone. "Mom?"

"Hello, honey."

"How are you?"

"Well, not too well right at the moment." Her voice sounded a little fuzzy, her words somewhat slurred.

Alarm rose in Ryanne's chest. "What's the matter?"

"I had a little accident."

"Are you all right? What's wrong?"

"I fell and broke my collarbone. I'm all bandaged up and in a hospital bed. It's quite undignified the way they have me trussed and dressed."

"Oh, my goodness! Well, how did this happen?" Nick had come to stand by her and listen. Ryanne placed her hand over the receiver and said, "She fell and broke her collarbone."

"I tripped over the hose, actually. I was watering my cactus."

"I didn't think you watered cactus."

"What?"

"Well, it's not important. Did you have someone to take you to the hospital? Did you call an ambulance?"

"Oh, no, no, my friend Gil brought me. He's here now."

"Oh. Well, Mom, I'll be there as soon as I can. I'll call and get a flight." Mentally, she tallied her bank balance and wondered if there'd be enough for a plane ticket.

"I'd like it if you came, Ryanne," her mother said. "I really would. I don't want to be a bother to you, though."

"Nonsense. What hospital are you in?"

She grabbed a pen and paper from the kitchen desk and jotted a location and phone number, then said her goodbyes and hung up.

Ryanne explained the situation to Mel and Nick. Ann Marie took the boys into the family room.

"Let me see what I can find online," Nick said, sitting in front of his computer and signing on.

Ryanne stood with her hip against the counter, feeling a little confused. Her thoughts traced over her responsibilities to Nick. "What about Jamie?" she said suddenly. "I promised I'd stay with him until his day care was ready."

"That's only another day or so," Nick told her.

Ann Marie had come to stand in the doorway. "Excuse me," she said hesitantly. "But I'd be more than happy to help with Jamie. I'm here, anyway, and you've all been so nice to me. My arm is much better. I can't go back to work yet, but I can sure look after Jamie. He and Dylan are good company for each other."

Nick turned back to the screen. "I think that's a great idea, Ann Marie. You and Dad can help me hold down the fort for a few days." He scrolled down a screen. "How about nine forty-five, Rye?"

"Tonight?"

"Yup." He reached into his back pocket, withdrew his wallet and entered a credit card number.

"What are you doing?"

"Buying a ticket."

Ryanne looked from Nick to Mel, then over at Ann Marie. They all seemed to take Nick's action in stride. "I can pay for my own ticket," she said.

"We'll worry about that later. This was quick." He printed out a receipt and signed off. "Better get packed. You'll need this."

"Nick…" she said softly. She glanced at the amount on the receipt and her stomach dropped.

Mel and Ann Marie busied themselves finishing the dishes.

Nick stepped into the dining room and she followed.

"Don't you want to go?" he asked.

Of course she wanted to go; that wasn't the problem. The problem was Nick stepping in and making plans for her—spending money she couldn't afford to pay back. It was dangerous to lean on someone, let anyone do things for her or be too supportive. It wouldn't do to let herself get used to it. She'd stood on her own two feet even when she was married. But for now, for the time being, she was very glad of Nick's assistance. "Yes, of course I do. Thanks for your help."

"Go home and pack. It's a two-hour drive."

Reaching the airport in Des Moines by nine, they shared a drink in the terminal lounge.

Nick sat beside Ryanne and held her hand. "Tell your mom her lawn looks good this summer."

"I told her that on the phone last week. She said you always take care of it for her. Lately, I've been wondering why she hasn't sold the place. I guess I never really paid any attention before...not ever being here. But now it seems...odd.''

''I don't know. She spends a few weeks here in the spring each year. And a few weeks in the fall. Maybe she just doesn't want to cut her ties.''

Ryanne would have been out of luck for a place to go if her mother *had* severed her ties to Elmwood. ''Maybe.''

''Got a pen?''

Ryanne dug one from her bag and handed it to him. He jotted something on a napkin. ''Here's my cell phone number.''

She folded the napkin with a grin and tucked it into her bag.

''What's so funny?''

She leaned forward and kissed him. ''You.''

All at once she realized how much she was going to miss him—and Jamie—and a lump came to her throat. She might as well get used to it; she'd have to leave them soon, anyway.

Nick walked her to her gate and she hugged him, an emptiness she'd never known before rising up inside her. She clung to him for a long moment, drew in the scent of his hair and his skin from a recent shave. She'd taken a lot of business trips over the years, boarded a good many planes, but she'd never felt lost at leaving someone behind.

This feeling was foolish; she'd only be gone a few days, and it wasn't as though she had a commitment to Nick in the first place. He was a friend. Well, friend wasn't quite an apt description anymore, but lover sounded too much like...love should be involved.

She gave her boarding pass to the attendant and walked through the doors toward the ramp. Seated and buckled in, she peered through the window at the enormous panes of glass of the terminal, spotted Nick's tall form and waved, though he probably couldn't see her.

Tears blurred her vision. Before long, she would be doing this for real. Leaving Nick and Iowa for good. The knowledge that her time in Elmwood would soon be behind her didn't rest as comfortably as it had years ago. Now, she wondered what exactly she had ever been running away from.

Careful of her mother's injuries, Ryanne greeted her with a kiss on the cheek. Evelyn Whitaker's shoulder was wrapped and her arm was bound securely to her chest, but she wore a warm smile when she saw her daughter. With her good hand, she grasped Ryanne's and kept her close by her side. "Your mother is a clumsy thing," she said.

"You got tangled in the hose, Mom?" Ryanne asked.

"I'm not even sure what happened. I tripped over a loop and fell against the concrete."

"The sidewalk?"

"Yes, or the porch step somehow. I don't know. They're getting ready to discharge me."

"Good. We'll get you settled at your place."

Ryanne helped handle all the paperwork and talked with the doctor, then phoned a cab.

"We could have called Gil," Evelyn said as they rode toward her home. "He drove me here."

"This is fine," Ryanne assured her. She'd had cash for the cab to the hospital and for this one, since Nick had paid for her plane fare. Now she had to pay him back somehow.

The small house with its rocky front yard and arid landscaping was foreign to Ryanne. She'd been there only once before. Her mother handed her the keys and she unlocked the door and ushered her in, then went back for their luggage, purses and two plants.

Evelyn was sitting on the sleek contemporary sofa, and had removed her shoes and raised her feet to the wrought-iron-and-glass coffee table. The furniture was ultramodern, the carpet white, a drastic contrast to the vintage look and feel of the home in Elmwood.

"Let me go get you a couple of pillows," Ryanne said. She found the bedroom, also decorated in an airy modern style, and glanced around. Being here made it feel as though she didn't even know her mother anymore. She didn't. She was a stranger in her mother's new life.

Carrying back two pillows, she helped Evelyn get settled in a reclining position with her feet up.

"That's nice, honey," her mother said. "Are you thirsty or hungry? We missed the hospital lunch, thank goodness."

"You'll let me take care of that."

Ryanne prepared sandwiches and made iced tea, and they ate while visiting. Even the kitchen had been filled with sleek modern appliances, not an antique in sight. "This is all so *different*, Mom. You don't have a single antique here."

Her mother looked around. "No."

"You used to take me antique shopping all the time, remember?"

Her mother nodded. "You enjoyed it so. There are several shops nearby if you'd like to see them. I don't know what they're like because I've never been to them, but we could find a few once I'm rested."

Ryanne gave her a curious glance. "Did your tastes change? You don't like antiques anymore?"

"I think they're nice. I just never loved them like you did. You were always fascinated by the history of the pieces."

Her reply was puzzling. Ryanne mulled it over, thought of the house full of furniture in Elmwood. "What about all the pieces at the house? The sideboards and tables and chairs and the clock...." Her mind catalogued the place.

"I guess I think of those as yours, dear. I couldn't bear to part with them unless you wanted to."

Ryanne took in this revelation with astonishment. "You bought all that stuff for me?"

"We bought it together. That's the history that means something to me."

Ryanne thought back over the trips she and her mother had taken while she'd been growing up. They'd always shopped and brought something home. Only now did she realize that each piece had been something that Ryanne herself had fallen in love with.

"Do you ever intend to live in Elmwood again, Mom?"

"I don't think so, honey. I'm very happy here. I moved to Elmwood with your father when he got a job at the college. You have your life in California, so there's really nothing there in Iowa for me anymore.''

"You've never sold the house."

"What would I do with all your furniture?" she said with a smile.

"Surely the property's a financial burden," Ryanne said.

"No. The house is paid for. The taxes are minimal. I only visit occasionally, certainly not enough to make the place worth keeping if you don't want it. If you don't want the furniture, we can store it, or have an auction," she said. "The pieces will bring a good price. Maybe it's time. While you're there, you can take the things you want."

Ryanne couldn't imagine selling that house. Even though she'd thought she wanted to get away from Elmwood, she'd always known the place was a refuge, somewhere safe and secure that would be waiting. "Do *you* want to sell the house?"

"Actually it's joint property, you know. Your name is on the deed."

"No, I'd forgotten."

"Half the money will be yours. Not that you care, I suppose, but you can invest it."

That information was good news and bad news rolled into one, creating a terrible quandary. If they sold it, she could use her half to pay on her debts. But how could she sell it? She'd cleaned and polished and reacquainted herself with the place, enjoying it like an old friend she'd missed.

How could she not? Selling it would solve a huge

problem. "Maybe I'll check with a Realtor when I get home. Back, I mean. When I get back."

That night Ryanne made herself a bed on the sofa, then tidied up. She carried a bag to her mother's room. Evelyn was sitting at her dressing table, working moisturizer into her skin with one hand.

"Let me set these down and I'll help you." Ryanne carried the toiletries into the bathroom and opened a narrow closet door. Men's shaving gear and cologne sat on the bottom shelf. She stared for a moment, then placed the items inside and closed the door.

She wasn't shocked, really. Her mother had been without a mate for years now. Certainly she needed her own life. But the fact that Evelyn hadn't shared this development hurt. It was Ryanne's own fault, she realized belatedly. She hadn't exactly shown an interest or spent any time keeping their relationship close.

She studied her mother, her hair colored a shiny dark gold as it always had been, her form slim and attractive, her eyes bright and intelligent. "What's your favorite fragrance, Mom?"

Her mom glanced at the small selection on her dressing table and picked up a bottle. "This one. Why?"

Ryanne took it and spritzed a little on her mother's wrists, then sniffed her. "Yes. It smells like you. I like it."

She took the brush and pulled it through Evelyn's silky tresses. "Who does your hair?"

"A hilarious young man with a goatee and an earring. He makes me laugh while he colors and cuts."

She blushed and waved her hand in front of her face. "Last time he asked me if I wanted a bikini wax, can you imagine?"

Hearing her mother talk about her hairdresser, Ryanne laughed. They chatted for a few minutes more, but eventually Evelyn grew weary. Ryanne brought her a pain pill and a glass of water, and tucked her into bed.

She perched on the side. "Tell me about Gil."

Her mother smoothed the covers with one hand. "He's a widower. A retired dentist. He has two spaniels and a Russian blue cat, so he pays someone to vacuum his carpet and furniture three times a week. He cooks much better than I do. In fact, he does a show on a local cable channel, giving cooking classes.

"And he loves people. He talks to people everywhere we go. Dresses up like a clown for the kids at the hospital."

Ryanne thought of her father, so suspicious of people's motives, concerned about appearances, definitely not a people person, and knew why her mother would appreciate someone just the opposite. "He sounds great. I can't wait to meet him."

"I told him you were coming. He offered to come cook for us tomorrow. I said I'd have to ask you. I didn't want to put you on the spot."

"I'd love to meet him," Ryanne said. "You tell him I'll be really hungry."

Evelyn grasped her daughter's hand. "Thank you, Ryanne. For coming."

"I'm really glad to be here." She blinked away tears, kissed her mom's cheek and stood. "I'm sorry

I haven't come to visit more often. From now on, I will."

"I'd like that."

"Me, too." Leaving the room, Ryanne pulled the door closed. From her makeshift bed, she dialed Nick's cell phone number.

On the second ring, he answered. "Miss you."

She smiled. "What were you doing?"

"Would you believe I'm lying here in bed naked, thinking about you?"

She glanced at the clock, remembering all the nights he'd stayed awake. "No. What were you really doing?"

"Tweaking an engine."

"Now that's sexy."

He chuckled. "How's your mom?"

"She's doing fine. She's home. Nick, she has a boyfriend."

"Yeah? A stud?"

"Knock it off. He's a really good friend to her. I think she likes him a lot."

"Well, that's great. Isn't it?"

"Yes. I think it is. How's Jamie?"

"Still in seventh heaven with a live-in buddy. They had to set up the tent tonight."

"Oh, no. No sleep for you." She was kidding, because she'd recognized that Jamie had little to do with Nick's not getting enough sleep.

"Ann Marie's on night watch."

"Nick," Ryanne said softly. She'd put all the evidence together. "I saw all the books by your reading chair."

"Uh-huh."

"Do you have a sleep disorder?"

He didn't answer and she feared she'd gone too far. She didn't share personal things with him, after all. She shouldn't have asked. She'd stepped over the line into something he had chosen not to tell her about. Silence stretched uncomfortably along the phone line.

Chapter Twelve

Finally, he said, "Insomnia."

"That must be miserable."

"It's getting better. I just have to practice the relaxation methods that work for me and keep a schedule. I can't sleep during the day or drink or smoke, which I don't do anyway. I need to get bright light during the day, keep a sleep journal—you didn't read that, did you?"

"No."

"And—don't laugh."

"I don't think this is a laughing matter."

"Well, I schedule worry time for during the day. I don't allow myself to worry at night."

"That's disciplined," she said, wondering like mad what it was he worried about.

"Actually, I'm not supposed to do anything in bed except sleep…but I make an exception for you."

"You mean sleeping with me?"

"No, I mean sex."

She laughed. "Well, the kitchen table would be a little uncomfortable."

He laughed, too, and then silence stretched between them. "Rye," he said softly.

"What?"

He paused a moment too long. "I, uh, miss you."

"I'll probably stay a few more days."

"Enjoy your time with your mom. Give her my love."

A little thrill of alarm went through her chest at his simple words. "I will."

"Night."

"Good night, Nick." She stared at her hand on the phone, felt the chugging of her heart at Nick's mention of the word *love*, even spoken so casually and in reference to her mother. Ryanne had the feeling he'd wanted to say something more to her. That terrified her.

Turning off the light, she snuggled under the sheet and lightweight blanket. Don't worry at night. That was a good theory, if you could put it into practice. In the depths of night, her mind sometimes drove her crazy with troubling thoughts and memories. What problems did Nick have to keep him awake? His life seemed so orderly, so simple, and he always seemed satisfied with it. Didn't he? Sure, maybe he regretted that his marriage hadn't worked out, but Ryanne had never picked up on any feelings that he was still grieving over his ex-wife.

His voice in her ear was still a tangible memory.

She closed her eyes and savored it. *I miss you.* Dangerous. Risky. Too much. Way too much.

Honest.

Nick was honest with her. With himself. He missed her. She couldn't even let herself return the thought. She couldn't afford to miss him. If she missed him now, she'd miss him more when she took a job and left. Nope, she wasn't going there.

Ryanne turned her thoughts to the job offers she'd received earlier in the week. After two promising phone interviews, she had narrowed her choice down. Now she vowed to make a decision on one of them before she went back to Elmwood. It was time to stop playing games and get back to real life. She'd been closing off reality for too long. Nick Sinclair wasn't part of her real life.

"Your mother told me you were beautiful, but I thought that was just a mother's biased opinion," Gil Redding said the next evening as they stood in the kitchen.

Ryanne blushed at the compliment. "Thank you."

"I hope you like blackened salmon." Gil tossed a colorful green salad and then served it up onto salad plates.

"I love salmon," Ryanne said.

"Good." He added mandarin oranges and slivered almonds and drizzled the salad with poppy seed dressing. "Want to set these on the table?"

"Everything is so pretty and smells wonderful." She and her mother took their places.

"I practice on your mother for my show. It's all

perfectly nutritious, you know. We watch our diet carefully.''

"I'm a healthy guinea pig," Evelyn said, giving him an adoring smile.

Gil placed the rest of the meal on the table and seated himself before he poured the wine.

"Ryanne is going to look into selling the house in Iowa," Evelyn told him.

"Are you sure you want to do that?" Gil looked from mother to daughter. "It's a nice vacation house, isn't it?"

"You've never been to Iowa in August, or you wouldn't say that." Evelyn placed her napkin on her lap. "There are only a few weeks a year when you don't have to run either the furnace or the air-conditioning."

"It hasn't been so bad this summer," Ryanne said somewhat defensively, and wasn't sure why. She'd perspired buckets in that upstairs bedroom.

"We might as well invest the money and let some nice family enjoy the house," Evelyn replied.

Her mother was perfectly correct. Without a doubt that's what they should do. "We might as well," Ryanne agreed. She shouldn't care. She hadn't been back to that house more than a day or two every couple of years until this summer. She was leaving, anyway. The place would only sit there unoccupied.

"I could go rent a movie for you ladies to watch this evening," Gil offered. "Anything you'd like to see?"

"Only if you stay and watch it with us," Ryanne replied.

"That would give me much pleasure, thank you," he said, obviously touched by her acceptance.

After he'd gone that night, Ryanne and her mother sat in the kitchen and had another glass of wine.

"I like him a lot," Ryanne told her.

"It must seem strange to you," Evelyn said. "Me being with another man."

"It does. But it seems right, too. I'm glad you're happy here. Fulfilled, you know. You deserve it after your life with Dad."

Her mother looked at her oddly. "Whatever do you mean?"

"I just mean you didn't really get a chance to live the life you wanted. Now you're free to do what you enjoy."

"I lived my life exactly as I wanted," her mother told her emphatically. "I liked being the wife of a college professor, and all the duties that went along with it."

"The volunteer positions? You liked those?"

"Yes! Of course I did. I would have stayed and finished out my life there if things had been different."

"If dad hadn't run off with another woman."

"Yes. But it happened that way, and I've moved on to another phase in my life."

"You weren't devastated by his betrayal?"

"Of course it hurt. But not like it would have if things had been better between us. He is not an easy man to love."

Her feelings in retrospect sounded oddly like Ryanne's feelings about Mason, now that she'd had time to consider and collect herself. She was still mad as hell, but she didn't miss him—or want him back—except to pay his debt to her.

"I think I feel that way about Mason, too," she said. "In fact, I don't know if I ever really did love him." She took a sip and swallowed. "Did you love Dad?"

"Yes, honey, I loved him very much once."

"Do you love Gil?"

Evelyn nodded. "Gil's easy to love."

These days with her mother had been the most enlightening Ryanne had ever spent. Her mother was not the unfulfilled woman she'd always believed. Why had Ryanne ever thought that? Her mother had been satisfied to make a home and perform the duties of a professor's wife and raise her daughter.

Ryanne's perceptions had obviously been skewed by her father's high opinion of himself and his position—and his low opinion of other people. In always wanting to better herself and rise above her life situation, had she taken on some of his haughtiness?

By the end of the week, her mother had visited the doctor and accompanied Ryanne on a shopping trip. Gil offered his services as cook and driver, and Ryanne felt comfortable leaving Evelyn in his care.

"I've enjoyed this time more than you can know," her mother told her as they waited for a cab to take Ryanne to the airport.

"I do know," Ryanne assured her. "I'm sorry that we haven't done this before. I was so wrapped up in my career that I let the really important things slide right past."

"Your career is important, honey."

"Not as important as the people I love."

"You're young. You have plenty of years to love and work your career in."

Ryanne didn't feel young anymore. She felt tired, and realized she had been for a while now. Her discontent had been sneaking up on her, and she'd been working harder and harder, trying to hide the fact. She had years left to feel like this?

The cab pulled up in front of the house.

Ryanne hugged her mom. "I love you."

Once in the back seat, she waved and wiped a tear from her cheek. What an eye-opening week this had been.

During the flight, she made a decision to accept a job. A pharmaceutical company in Albany had offered her a position as head of their marketing department. The salary was what she needed to tackle the remaining debt and start over. An advance bonus would take care of the IRS for another six months and give her the means to set up an apartment. Perhaps the house would sell sometime soon, too.

Resolving to call them when she got back gave her only minimal relief. She'd made a choice, but it gave her no gratification.

Knowing how busy Nick was, she'd hated to ask him to meet her, but she needed a ride home. He was waiting for her in the terminal, and with his dark hair swept back from his forehead, wearing a short-sleeved knit shirt and a new-looking pair of jeans, he'd never looked better. She took a deep breath and mentally prepared herself for the loss that was to come.

Nick's sunglasses were tucked into his shirt pocket

and pressed into her shoulder when he hugged her. "Good flight?"

With a nod, she pulled away and headed for the luggage carousel.

Nick carried her bag to his car, a Crown Victoria with tinted windows and glorious air-conditioning.

"I saw this car parked out back." She buckled her seat belt.

"This is Dad's. I knew you'd want to keep cool."

"Arizona was refreshing compared to this."

"Heat index was a hundred and five yesterday. I had your air-conditioners checked out. They're running now. Only a little low on freon."

She turned toward him. "You shouldn't have done that."

"I knew you hadn't gotten around to it."

"But I didn't ask you to take that on."

"I did it as a favor. No big deal."

"Give me the bill when we get there."

"It wasn't that much—"

"I want the bill, Nick."

"Okay. All right. I was just being neighborly."

"No, you were butting in where you didn't belong."

He said nothing, driving with his gaze straight ahead.

Ryanne watched the countryside roll past. Her reaction probably seemed out of line, but he had no idea that she was living on a shoestring budget for the time being. "How is Ann Marie doing?"

"She's fine."

"How's—"

"Jamie's fine. Dad's fine."

Ryanne sat speechless for a minute, then turned to look at him. He was angry. "I'm going to put the house up for sale," she announced.

"Your mom's house?"

"It's half mine."

A muscle in his jaw clenched. He relaxed his hands on the steering wheel and gave her a sidelong look. "I see."

What did he see? That she was distancing herself from him right here and now? That she should never have let things between them go as far as they had? That now she had to pull herself together and go on with her life?

They barely spoke the rest of the way home. Nick pulled into his driveway and parked the Ford in the shade beside the house. He got her bags from the trunk.

She reached for them, but he moved past her, carrying them toward her mother's house. Her lawn had been mowed recently.

"You mowed?"

"Actually, Forrest Perry did it this week. He heard about your mom's accident and that you were going to see her. Jon Langley came by and worked on the rose trellises and pulled weeds."

"What did they do that for?"

He set her bags on the shaded porch while he waited for her to climb the stairs. Then he gave her a penetrating look. "They wanted to do something to help. You see a sinister motive in that, too?"

"Of course not." She moved forward.

"No one can be nice to you, because it destroys

the myth than everyone is out to get you, is that it? Nobody's just genuinely caring and helpful.''

"Stuff it, Nick."

He stayed right behind her. "Are you in some sort of trouble?"

Her steps faltered, then she continued across the porch. "That's an odd question. What sort of trouble would I be in?"

"I don't know—you tell me. You're just awfully secretive and..."

"And what?"

"And you're always holding out."

She stared at him, speechless.

"You always hold a little something back," he said. "And it's because of this. Because you're leaving. You're getting ready to go, aren't you? Just like you've always planned. Running just like you've always run."

She nodded. "You knew I'd be going."

He turned to leave, but stopped halfway down the stairs. "So did you, damn it. So did you."

She couldn't bear to look into his eyes. She lowered her gaze.

He moved down the stairs and was gone.

Ryanne unlocked the door and carried her bags in. The entry and living room were surprisingly cool.

Her mail was stacked on the inlaid table beneath a gilt-framed mirror. She couldn't imagine this table and mirror anywhere but here. They'd been here for as long as she could remember. The brass vase had been a flea market purchase one hot fall day, and now she remembered her mother buying it at her suggestion. Ryanne glanced up, saw her reflection and recognized the agonized expression on her face. She looked away.

Walking through the downstairs rooms, she mentally cataloged each piece, remembering when and where it had been purchased. But she couldn't picture the house without a single one of them.

She would show the house first, get that out of the way, before she worried about what to do with the collection of furnishings and accessories.

The look that had been in Nick's eyes haunted her. She couldn't help disappointing him. Was she supposed to feel guilty for taking a few weeks of happiness for herself? He'd known what he was getting into. *So had she,* he'd made a point of telling her.

She worked up a measure of anger in order to dispel the yawning emptiness in the area of her heart. He had promised to be her friend. *Promised.*

Her control slipping, Ryanne walked to the kitchen and got a glass from the cupboard. As she stood in front of the freezer, Jamie's Sunday school picture caught her attention. Daniel in the lion's den. Jamie had told her to keep it so she'd remember not to be afraid. She touched the brightly colored artwork, smiled because she knew Jamie stuck his tongue out the corner of his mouth when he concentrated, and that he probably had when he'd colored this.

Sometimes you just couldn't help being afraid. A tear slipped down her cheek. Life was so full of risks that deferring to caution was the only way to avoid big mistakes.

She should have remembered that before she let Nick get too close. Now she didn't know which frightened her more—the thought of leaving, or the fact that she wasn't sure she wanted to anymore.

Nick had explained to Jamie that Ryanne was tired from her trip and needed to rest, but still his son had driven him crazy with questions about when he could go over and see her.

Ann Marie had been offered a furnished apartment over the hardware store, and Nick felt comfortable with her staying there, what with Eddie having trouble getting bail. Even once he got out, she had a restraining order, and she'd be close to people and near enough to walk to her job at the Three B's. With Nate Keenan, who owned the building, Nick helped Ann Marie move her things and get settled. Birdy, who worked at the hardware store, helped, too, promising Nick she'd keep an eye on Ann Marie and Dylan.

"How's Ryanne?" she asked. "I haven't talked to her since she came home."

They were standing at the foot of the stairs. Nick opened the door, which led onto the street beside the store. It had grown late while they were moving boxes, and the streetlights were on. "She's selling the house, so she's keeping busy getting it spruced up."

"Oh." Birdy seemed surprised. "Where's she going?"

"Back to California."

"Oh. Well, I'll give her a call."

Nick's phone rang. "Sinclair."

"Harold Clement heard a shot and his yard light's out," Nick's dispatcher, Sharon, said.

Nick grimaced and held the phone away to cuss.

"I heard that," Sharon said.

"I'd rather chase turkeys than go over there and listen to his tirade again."

"Want me to send Duane?"

"No. I'm all over it." He returned the phone to his belt as he walked toward the cruiser at the curb. "Tell Ann Marie I have a call, okay?" he called over his shoulder.

"You've been a big help to her, Nick," Birdy said sincerely.

"She's helping herself now. That's what matters," he replied.

"Don't take any credit."

"I don't."

She waved him off. "Go fight crime, Inspector."

As soon as Nick arrived at the Clement place, he barked at the bystanders to get the hell home, and listened to the cranky pharmacist ranting on about the expense of replacing glass and bulbs.

"You're supposed to be doing something about this!" Harold shouted. "You're the law around here, and my yard is being vandalized. I can't even claim it on my insurance because the deductible is two hundred dollars."

"Maybe if you didn't alert the whole damned neighborhood and have them trampling evidence into the ground before I got here, I'd have something to go on."

"Get the crime lab out here."

"This isn't a homicide investigation, Harold."

"Yet!"

"Oh, for—" Nick ignored him to fill out a report.

"A lot of good all that paperwork does."

Nick completed the report.

Apparently finished grumbling without an audience, Harold went into his house and slammed the door.

Nick tossed the clipboard into the cruiser, switched on his flashlight and directed the beam across the trampled grass. Jamie was at home with Mel, both fast asleep by now; Ryanne was finished with him and going back to her illustrious life; he hadn't a prayer of sleeping, so he might as well make himself useful, even if it was too dark to see anything.

Ryanne had always been an elusive butterfly. She'd always been older, smarter, independent...always the unattainable fantasy. He should have matured enough to get over a teenage crush and realize she wasn't for him.

But it wasn't a crush. What he felt for her was bone deep. Passion, yes. But love, too. Love as he'd never felt for another woman. He wanted her still. And he would never have her. She was as unattainable as always. He'd shared physical bliss with her; she'd given him that much. But he still didn't have her, not really. He never had.

His chest ached with dawning insight and acceptance. Even when they'd been as intimately close as possible, she'd held herself back—the part of herself he truly craved: her heart. He was merely a convenience for her, a little side attraction while she was on vacation.

Nick had been walking aimlessly, scanning the grass and bushes and flowerbeds with the beam of light. Something glittered, and he moved the light back to find it again, then walked closer. He'd traveled all the way to the house next door while pondering his dilemma of the heart, and what had caught his attention lay on the ground right beside old lady Pascal's enormous front porch.

Nick shined the beam at what appeared to be casings. Brass shell casings.

He glanced up at the dark house, then bent and scooped them up. Half a dozen or more empty casings from a .22 lay in his palm. Dropping them into his pocket, he switched off the light and headed for the cruiser.

"Don't we have a Polaroid around here somewhere?" he asked Duane, once he'd arrived at the station.

"Can't get film for it anymore. There's a digital in the drawer back there."

Nick found the camera, placed the shell casings on a piece of paper and snapped a couple of shots. "You know how to send these pictures?"

"Sure. I have plenty of time to play with the toys on the night shift."

"Good. Send them to the state boys and see what they think."

Duane picked up a casing and examined it. "Where'd you find these?"

"I'm not saying until I get a response. And don't tell anyone."

Duane tossed it back and held up a palm defensively. "I won't."

"If they get back to you before I come in the morning, call."

"Roger. Night, boss."

The clock on the dash read 1:10 a.m. when he turned off the ignition. Nick got out of the car and locked it. Fireflies danced in front of him as he made his way to the back door.

"You said you'd be my friend."

Her voice startled him. Nick made out Ryanne's form on the cushioned glider that sat on the deck. "Rye."

She got up and moved toward him. "You said you'd be my friend, Nick, no matter what. You promised that getting more involved wouldn't spoil that."

He remembered making that promise in the heat of the moment. Maybe he'd really thought he could keep it. Being merely her friend had always been too hard. "We can go back to being friends like before," he said. "You live and work and have a life in California, and I live and work here. We see each other once every five years or so. It worked until now."

The only light came from the moon and a florescent bulb above the sink inside the kitchen, which gave a meager glow through the curtain at the window. He made out her features, but her expression was unreadable.

"Actually, I'm not going back to California," she said.

He moved closer to the glider and sat on the lawn chair across from her. Hope surged up in his chest like a volcano ready to explode. She was staying? He kept his voice calm. "You're not?"

"No. I've accepted a position in Albany. Doing marketing for a pharmaceutical company."

As quickly as hope had surged up, it plunged back down, taking any remaining good humor with it. "New York? That's quite a change. What about your agency?"

"I've sold it."

"When did you have time to do that?" She'd been here for a few weeks and had gone to her mother's for only a few days.

"I sold it before I came here."

And she'd never said a word. Never shared a glimpse of her life with him. "Why are you telling me now?"

"I want to keep in touch. See you and Jamie from time to time. You should know where I am, I guess."

"Maybe it's better if we just call it quits, Rye, and not pretend that it's going to be comfortable trying to stay friends."

She stood. "You promised."

"It was an unfair thing to make me promise."

"So this is it? Fine." Ryanne hurried down the wooden stairs before she started to cry. She'd got along without a friend until now; she could do it again. She should never have come over here.

"I'm not the one who made the rules and set the limits," he called after her.

"Lower your voice. The neighbors already watch me like hawks."

He caught up with her, but she kept going. "You're the one who wanted it this way. Nice and friendly. No strings. I was a good ride, better than your ten times with old Mason, and now you're ready to move on with your glamorous career and your life in the fast lane."

She stopped and swung at him, but he caught her wrist. "Are you jealous of my career?" she asked. "Is that it? You stayed here and married Holly because 'it was the right thing to do,' but it turned out to be the wrong thing. You never wanted more than this, and now you're sorry?''

''You don't know what I wanted,'' he said, his voice low and angry.

She jerked her arm away and continued toward the house, up the porch stairs and through the door. She didn't have a chance to close it, because he was still right behind her.

''You don't have a clue what I wanted, Rye.'' She'd left a light on in the living room and the anger in his face was clearly revealed.

Ryanne took a step back, daring him to tell her, to say something she didn't know—or maybe only suspected. ''What did you want, Nick?''

Chapter Thirteen

This had always been a sore spot between them—her ambition, his seeming lack of. The unfamiliar look in his eyes frightened her. She wanted him to understand, to forgive her, to hold her and make her world stop spinning out of control.

"It's not like you said," she managed to say past a throat constricted with tears. "It was never just a good time with you, Nick. It was good—it was wonderful...but it meant something. To me, it meant something. This is what I never wanted to happen. This—" she gestured to the space between them "—this awful, God, this *awful* hurt and these words we'll regret."

His expression changed, softened. He ran a hand down his face and cupped his chin for a moment, all the while studying her with eyes full of mistrust and disappointment. She'd done that to him. She'd disappointed him.

Crossing the space between them, she took his hand from his face and replaced it with her own, touching the faint, scratchy evening beard, his silky dark hair, and those lips that gave such ecstasy when they made love. He caught her against him with both arms and lowered his mouth.

His kiss burned her lips and demanded she surrender to his urgency. Ryanne wrapped her arms around his neck and kissed him fiercely, matching his ardent energy, wanting much more of him, but knowing that this would be all they had.

She ground herself against him, eager for the intimacy and solace within reach. Without breaking the kiss, Nick reached for the fastening of her shorts. She unbuttoned his shirt and pushed it down over his shoulders, but he didn't release her to let it drop. He had her shorts down and she kicked them away, let him lower her to the carpet, and tried to keep him close while he tugged his jeans down.

He took her there on the floor, the urgent coupling a release and a bond at the same time. Poised at the edge of fulfillment, Ryanne held Nick close and cried silently against his salty skin. The waves of pleasure and desolation crashed together, both depleting her mental and physical reserves.

When Nick lay still, nothing but his labored breathing making a sound in the room, she pressed her lips against his neck. He rolled to the side, pulled up his pants and gathered her against him, stroking her bare hip.

The window unit whirred on, brushing a breeze

across their heated bodies. Nick offered her his arm for a pillow. Finally, after what seemed a long peaceful time later, he said, "Rye?"

"Hmm?"

"Are you selling the house because you need money?"

She stiffened in his arms, and she knew he felt it. "Why do you think that?"

"I'm not Magnum, but I did get an obvious clue or two." He brushed her hair from her shoulder. "You're selling your car. Now you're selling the house. Apparently, you sold your business."

Ryanne's entire body burned with humiliation. She sat up, found her shorts and scrambled into them, facing away from him.

"I thought maybe, if you'd let me, I could help you out. I have a little money."

Her worst nightmare was unfolding—worse than losing the business and her self-respect, worse then losing Nick as a friend. Now he'd know her secret shame. Her blood pounded in her ears. "Even if that was true, why would you want to help me?"

"Because I care," he answered simply.

"Even if it was true and you had enough money to give me—it could be a huge amount, you don't know—it could be possible that I couldn't begin to pay it back for a good long time. But trust me, Nick, you don't know what you're offering."

"So it's a lot of money?"

She hadn't denied it. She'd walked right into his questions unprepared and hadn't had a response to satisfy his curiosity. She got to her feet and straightened her clothing. "Okay, I owe a lot of money. There."

Nick sat up. "Let me help you."

"We're talking tens of thousands here, not a few hundred in a savings account."

Something flared in his eyes. "Okay."

"Close to a hundred grand." That ought to send him running.

"Okay. It's yours."

She stared down at him. "You have a hundred grand."

"Yes."

"And you'd give it to me."

"Sure."

"Why?"

"It's only money. If I can't use it to help the people I—I care about, what good is it?"

"Where did you get a hundred grand to throw away?" she asked, completely baffled.

His tightened jaw revealed his irritation with the question. He got up and moved to the edge of the sofa. "I've done pretty well with my little hobby," he said sarcastically.

"Fixing cars?"

"Restoring classics. Making customized parts for collectors."

"You're serious?"

He nodded. "You know those magazines you saw in my room?" At her nod, he went on. "If you'd looked closely, you'd have seen my cars and parts featured. I have a Website I sell from, too."

Ryanne couldn't have been more surprised if he'd told her he'd discovered a cure for cancer. All along,

Nick had been building a profitable business from his home right here in Elmwood. He was a success, more of a success than she'd ever been. And he hadn't sacrificed his family or his integrity.

She mulled over the irony. "So, if you have a successful business, profiting from something you obviously enjoy more than being a sheriff, why are you still chasing turkeys and locking up drunks?"

He leaned his head against the back of the sofa and closed his eyes. "You want to get right to the grit, don't ya?"

Not to be put off, she settled on a footstool.

"As long as it's not you spilling your guts, you get right to the point," he added, but she said nothing, simply waited. After a minute, Nick raised his head and looked at her. "My dad thought it would be a wise decision. He needed me. The work was steady. It was an income before I had anything else established. Once I had so many years in, got promoted, I was obligated to so many people that I just couldn't back out."

"You became the sheriff to please your father. You married Holly because it was the right thing. Why was it the right thing, Nick? Was she pregnant?"

"No!" He shook his head and frowned. "Hell, no. I never touched her until after we were married."

"Then why? Did you love her?"

"I thought I could love her. I thought she needed someone."

At that moment, it all started making sense. "Because of Justin," she said softly.

He nodded. Then stood. "You always manage to

turn it around so that I'm the one on the hot seat, have you ever noticed?''

"Nick, you've spent your whole life trying to please other people, trying to take care of everybody. When are you going to take care of yourself?''

He shook his head as though he didn't know the answer.

Ryanne got up and went to him, wrapping her arms around his waist and hugging him. "Thank you for offering to help me. I can't take your money. This is something I have to get out of myself.''

"What happened?''

"I made a mess of things. Didn't pay close enough attention to finances and got wiped out. But I can start over. And I can do it on my own.''

He took a step back, let his arms fall to his sides and kept his gaze carefully averted. "Yes, I'm sure you can.''

He kissed her, a sad, yet sweet kiss, rubbed his knuckle against her cheek as though savoring last moments, then turned and left.

She'd made a mess of things, all right. Not only in her marriage and partnership with Mason, but in her relationship with Nick. If she'd wanted a friend, she should never have let herself fall into the delight of physical pleasures with him. They'd shared something above and beyond friendship, something that couldn't be easily forgotten or left behind.

She'd been seeking a place for herself for so long, and she'd thought she'd found it at the agency. But the work had never been as fulfilling as she'd thought it should be. The supposed successes of her past paled beside her recent experiences with her mother and the

Sinclairs. She'd felt important. Accepted. She'd felt as though she belonged. The Sinclairs, Birdy, everyone here had accepted her for who she was—or who she was pretending to be. A pang of guilt struck her once again.

She'd learned that she didn't have to strive to be better and better, or to prove anything—or knock herself out to become the person her father thought she should be. Elmwood no longer represented an obstacle to overcome. The town and its citizens had somehow come to mean peace and contentment.

This time when she left, she would be leaving something she truly cared about behind.

Nick stared at the stack of work on his desk. On top was a folder that he'd been opening, then closing and ignoring, for most of the week. Finally, he took out all the data and reports and looked them over again.

"I got findings back on those bullet casings," he told Bryce.

"What'd they say?"

"Pretty vague. Shells from a .22, as we knew. I'm going to go visit Mrs. Pascal today."

"Old lady Pascal?"

Nick nodded. "I want you to come with me."

Bryce's grin inched up one side of his mouth. "You need backup, boss?"

"I need a diversion."

"You think the old gal has a .22 she's firing?"

"Those casings were under her porch railing, so it's likely. Her husband could have had an army issue weapon, or something for target practice. Even a squirrel gun.''

''What do you want me to do?''

''I don't know. Have her show you her roses or something. Give me some time to look around her house.''

''You don't have a search warrant.''

''Actually, I do. But I don't want to frighten her by going in like a SWAT team.''

Bryce grumbled, but he accompanied Nick to Marguerite Pascal's home.

''What a delightful surprise,'' she said, and welcomed them in. The house smelled of aged wood and ginger. The plump little woman wore a floral print house dress and an apron, like Nick remembered his grandmother always wearing. ''You're just in time for fresh cookies.''

Reluctance fleeing, Bryce raised his eyebrows and cheerfully followed her into the living room. Nick glanced around, seeing only vases and doilies and old black-and-white photographs.

''Follow her and keep her in there,'' Nick mouthed.

Bryce trailed Mrs. Pascal to the dining room and through a highly polished swinging door. Ryanne would love this place, he thought, looking around at the vintage furnishings. Everything he did made him think of her, it seemed, and he pushed away the ache and focused on his job.

Once alone, he opened drawers and Mrs. Pascal's sewing box, peeked inside an old phonograph player, then made his way into the dining room. Several china cabinets and a marble-topped sideboard were possible hiding places, but he didn't have time to look through any of them before the door swung out and Bryce, carrying a tray, preceded Mrs. Pascal.

"Is this your husband?" Nick asked, pointing to a picture on the wall, as though he'd been absorbed in it all along.

"Yes, that's my dear Gerald. He was a fine figure of a man, wasn't he?"

"He was a handsome man," Nick agreed. "He was a veteran, wasn't he? Seems I remember him carrying the flag in the Memorial Day parades every year."

"Oh, yes. We were married only weeks before he went to war. Come have a cookie." She handed him a glass of tea and an embroidered linen napkin.

Nick and Bryce munched warm ginger cookies and listened to her rattle on about Norm Turner discontinuing items she'd bought in his store for as long as she could remember. "Says he doesn't sell enough to keep it in stock," she said indignantly. "Now why wouldn't powdered starch sell?"

"Maybe because if anyone irons these days, they buy the spray kind?" Bryce offered.

"I tell you, women these days don't know how to keep a house and do laundry. Not like in my day. They waste time watching nonsense on the television and serve their families food filled with preservatives. Why, they're too lazy to even teach their children to tie their shoes and instead buy them shoes with Velcro!"

"Times have changed, haven't they?" Nick said in sympathy. "I haven't seen anyone who can grow roses like yours, Mrs. Pascal. Nobody cares to put in the time anymore. Have you seen them, Officer Olson?"

Bryce took his cue. "No, but I'd like to take a gander. Did you win a blue ribbon this year?"

He got up and Mrs. Pascal ushered him toward the door.

"I'll just take my time on these cookies, if you don't mind," Nick said. "They taste just like my grandmother used to make."

"Now there was a woman who could cook," the silver-haired matron said to Bryce.

The minute the two were on the porch, Nick got up and investigated closets and drawers. In a small room with a narrow bed and a freezer, he discovered a gun cabinet. Inside were a couple of rifles and an English-made Walther. Nick opened the unlocked cabinet and checked both the rifles. The cagey old woman had been shooting out Harold Clement's yard light.

When Bryce followed her back into the house fifteen minutes later, three boxes of cartridges were lying on the mahogany table beside the serving tray. Mrs. Pascal stopped short when she saw them.

"I'm taking all the bullets, Mrs. Pascal," Nick said. "It's not safe for you to be shooting at Harold's yard light. Someone could be seriously hurt. Or killed. And you wouldn't want that, would you?"

The old woman looked confused for a moment, then settled herself regally in her chair, which had crocheted doilies arranged on the arms and back. "I asked Harold a dozen times to move that light where it didn't shine in my bedroom window. I like to have my window open for fresh air at night, and that light shines right in my eyes. People don't get enough fresh air anymore, you know. Houses are all closed up. More and more children have asthma because of it.''

"If Harold's light gets broken again, he'll press charges against you. You don't want that.''

"I have enough trouble sleeping without that damned light shining in my face.''

"If I promise to do something so that the light doesn't shine in your face anymore, will you promise to lock that cabinet and leave the guns alone?''

She picked at a thread on her apron before agreeing. "Yes.''

Nick went through the dining room into her bedroom and glanced around. Through the lace-draped window, he could see Harold's lamppost.

"You should try lying here at night,'' said Mrs. Pascal, who had followed him. "You don't know how hard it is to get old and have trouble sleeping.''

"I can only imagine,'' Nick replied, truly sympathizing.

Bryce stood behind her, wearing an amused look.

"Mrs. Pascal,'' Nick said. "I'll do something about the glare from the light. I have an idea. But if you'd let Officer Olson and I move your bed over to this wall, the light wouldn't be directly in your line of vision.''

"My bed's been right here for forty years and I don't see any reason to move it now.''

"There's your reason.'' Nick pointed out the window. "If you want Harold to compromise, you're going to have to take a step, too.''

She waved her hand in disgust. "I have a loaf of banana bread to put in the oven. If you want to bust a gusset moving my bed, you go right ahead.''

Half an hour later, the cartridges safely locked away, Nick called every retailer in the county who sold ammunition and told them not to sell anything to Marguerite Pascal.

Birdy called Ryanne and stopped by for a glass of lemonade that evening. The temperature had dropped significantly, so they sat on the porch. "Sure looks strange," Birdy said, commenting on the For Sale sign in the front yard.

Ryanne had been uncomfortable ever since the sign had gone up the previous afternoon.

"You sure you want to sell the place?"

She didn't, not really. Taking the steps to have the house listed and having people look at it seemed all wrong. But she didn't have any avenues left to her. "It's the practical thing to do," she replied.

"Did you hear the news?" Birdy asked.

"What news?"

"Nick caught the culprit who was shooting out Harold Clement's yard light."

"No, who?"

"Old lady Pascal."

"Oh dear." Ryanne remembered the woman well. Mrs. Pascal had been a cafeteria worker when Ryanne was in grade school. "What's going to happen to her?"

"Nothing. Nick gave her a stern warning and took away her bullets. He also moved her bed so that the light didn't shine in her eyes, and last I heard he was planting a bush at the edge of the Clements' yard. To obstruct the view, but it will take awhile to grow, I'd think. I guess he talked to Harold about putting something instead of glass in the side of the lamp fixture that faces Mrs. Pascal's house.''

"That sounds like Nick.''

"Yeah, it does. Elmwood is lucky to have someone like him who cares about the people.''

Ryanne nodded. "People have been very good to me since I've been here.''

"They're always good to me,'' Birdy replied. "Oh, I get annoyed sometimes—the lack of privacy, you know—but that's just what comes with small-town life.''

"I guess.''

"Sort of like a big extended family. Sometimes they smother you, but they're always there when you need them.''

Ryanne glanced over to where Audrey Milligan was watering her petunias. The older woman waved and smiled, and Ryanne waved back. Today she wore a pair of yellow polyester pants and tennis shoes with flashing red lights in the heels. "Audrey sent my mom a plant,'' she said.

"They were neighbors for a lot of years,'' Birdy replied.

Ryanne glanced at the trellis that Jon Langley had repaired, and her lawn, which Forrest Perry had mowed during her absence. She'd learned that there was a volunteer group working to turn the Sunday school rooms at the First Presbyterian Church into a temporary day care. In fact, she'd been called to help shop for dishes and supplies with Natalie Perry.

Like a big family, was how Birdy had put it, and for the first time Ryanne saw the truth in that comparison. The citizens of Elmwood had always offered her mother help, especially after her father had left and Evelyn had been on her own for the first time. Ryanne's perception of the community had been skewed by her own sense of self-importance. The people were basically warm and welcoming, and she'd rejected that friendliness as prying.

Nick's patrol car pulled into the shade behind his house.

Ryanne's heart fluttered foolishly, and she looked away. "How is Ann Marie doing?"

"She's set up in the apartment over the hardware store. I check on her a couple of times a day. That Dylan is going to be a heartbreaker in a few more years, have you noticed?"

Ryanne nodded. That meant Mel was once again left to watch Jamie all day until the day care was ready. Guilt bored into her conscience. She'd promised to help. She'd wanted to help.

A while later, Birdy said her goodbyes and left. Ryanne set their glasses in the sink and walked through the house. She was going through a stack of papers when the phone rang.

"Ryanne, it's Lisa Crenshaw."

"Hi." She greeted the Realtor with whom she'd listed the house.

"I have a couple of people who want to look at the house tomorrow."

Ryanne's heart sank. "Okay."

"I'll show it at eleven and again at two."

"I'll be gone," she replied.

"All right then, hon. This is going to be a snap. It's a grand old house, and I always have people looking for something in that price range. I'll bet we have it sold within the week.''

"Thanks, Lisa." Ryanne hung up. She'd already been thinking she needed to let Nick know she would help with Jamie again. This call had made it easier, since she needed to be out of the house. Things were so tense between her and Nick that talking to him and seeing him was uncomfortable.

Memories of their last argument flooded her mind, and she recalled vividly the way they had kissed and touched and made love on the floor. Her gaze was drawn to the living room carpet, and heat washed up her body to her cheeks. She didn't want to be at odds with Nick. She'd never wanted that. It had been unrealistic to think they could become intimately involved and still keep their friendship intact. It had been unfair of her to make him promise.

But, oh, she missed him. She missed the heated energy in his eyes when he looked at her; she missed the way he said her name, the drives they'd taken…the nights they'd spent in each other's arms.

Swallowing the burning in her throat and the threat of tears, she ran up to freshen her face and hair, then crossed the lot between their homes. Hopefully, she'd given him time to finish his supper, though it was already dark. He'd arrived home late.

Ryanne knocked tentatively on the back door.

Nick opened it.

Seeing him, she regretted coming. She could have phoned. His hair was wet from a recent shower. His soft worn jeans molded to his legs and hips so sexily that her mouth went dry.

Nick stepped back to invite her inside without saying a word.

She glanced around.

"Dad's in his room and Jamie's watching TV."

"Oh." She glanced at the open dishwasher. She'd apparently interrupted a task. "I wanted to let you know I'd be over tomorrow. To stay with Jamie."

"You don't have to. I don't expect you to."

"Why not? I told you I would."

"Things have changed, haven't they?"

"They still aren't ready to open the day care. Mel shouldn't have to handle him all day and then be on call at night, too."

Nick's expression changed, and she knew she'd touched a vulnerable spot.

"And I want to do it," she added. "Those things haven't changed." She paused and said more softly, "I miss him."

"He misses you, too, but he's going to have to get used to it."

That hurt. She buried the pain deep before she spoke. "Not tonight, he doesn't. And not tomorrow. So I'll be here with him just as we planned before I went to my mom's."

Nick moved to finish the dishes. Finally, he said over his shoulder, "All right. Go on in and see him if you'd like."

Jamie jumped up from the cars he was playing with and met her with a huge smile and a hug. "Hi, Rye," he said, having picked up the nickname from his dad. "Dad said you was restin' from your trip to your mom's."

"I'm all rested," she said, and joined him on the floor.

"I hope nobody buys your house," he said. "'Cause then you won't have to leave."

"I'd still have to leave, Jamie. I'd just have less money. I have to go back to work."

"Can't you work here? My dad could pay you to watch me. I'd be pretty good most of the time."

She ran her hand over his shiny hair and kissed his temple. "It's not quite that simple, honey. Adults have bills to pay, and mine require me to take a job that pays a lot of money."

"Oh." He made a few engine noises as he raced a car across the edge of the trunk. He seemed to accept that explanation, and apparently didn't resent her for leaving, like his father did. She read him a book, and when Nick came into the room, she felt him studying the two of them.

Ryanne looked up and met his gaze.

"He's asleep," Nick said quietly.

She had noticed Jamie's weight against her shoulder. She laid down the book, careful to support Jamie's head.

"I'll carry him upstairs." Nick bent to scoop up his son, and Ryanne followed.

"Do I have to brush my teeth, Daddy?" Jamie sleepily poked his arms through the oversize T-shirt his dad slipped over his head.

"Yes, you do. I'll help you."

Ryanne sat on the edge of the narrow bed and waited for them to return. She tucked Jamie under the covers, kissed his forehead, and Nick turned out the light before giving him a hug. "Will you be here tomorrow?" Jamie asked Ryanne.

"I'll be here when you wake up."

"Okay. We can check on the anthill."

"That sounds like fun."

Nick and Ryanne stood in the hall for a moment, the silence between them awkward. Only a short time ago, she would have joined him in his bedroom and they would have...

He was thinking the same thoughts; she recognized the heat when he met her eyes in the meager glow of a night-light.

Nick turned his attention away, working hard to swallow his frustration and hurt. He descended the stairs, and she followed. He picked up miniature cars and stored them in a vinyl case under an end table, then walked toward the kitchen. He had a couple of hours left to work on a project—try to keep his mind occupied.

"I'm going out to the garage for a while."

"I guess I'll leave," she said. She walked out the back door ahead of him and crossed the lot.

Nick made his way to his garage and flipped on the lights and fans. He'd been thinking about everything she had said to him the other day. She hadn't understood his willingness to give up his own dreams to take care of Holly and his father, and then Jamie. Had he really been unfair to himself and to his family by stifling the things he really wanted?

Ryanne thought he'd be a more fulfilled person if he saw to his own desires instead of trying to please everyone else.

Maybe she was right. Maybe it was time he went

after what he wanted. He'd thought for days about what he wanted. And somehow none of it mattered without Ryanne in his life. She had become what he wanted.

He'd denied himself that admission in the past, and he was doing it again.

The door opened and he looked up from the workbench. Ryanne stood just inside the threshold. She glanced around. "I wanted to say something."

What could she say at this point that would make a difference? "Okay."

"I'm sorry, Nick. Sorry for being selfish. I've always gone after what I wanted at the risk of everything else. I really needed you this summer. I wanted what we shared, and I didn't let myself think of the consequences. I would never deliberately hurt Jamie, I hope you believe that. And I never wanted to hurt you. So...I'm sorry."

Years ago she had come to him in the old garage, leaned on a fender and wished him goodbye before she'd left for college. He'd been a boy of sixteen. Silently, not speaking what was in his heart, he'd watched her go. And he'd regretted it ever since.

He wouldn't make the same mistake again.

There were so few things he'd ever really wanted for himself. But Ryanne was one of them. Always had been. He laid down the part and the catalog he was holding and faced her squarely.

"Ryanne. I love you."

Chapter Fourteen

She stared at him, her eyes round and filled with confusion. A flush stained her cheeks. Nick's heart beat a mile a minute, the words he'd blurted hanging in the air between them.

"Stay and marry me," he said, walking closer. "We can take care of the debt you owe together."

Her mouth opened and closed twice before she pushed any words out. He wanted to reach for her, pull her close, but her expression was unreadable, keeping him at arm's length. Finally, she said, "This is my own mess, Nick. I have to work it out on my own."

"The hell with that," he answered, trying to keep from getting angry. "I can take care of your debts. I told you that."

Her rigid posture betrayed her negative reaction to

his proposal. "You're trying to take care of me, Nick," she said. "It's what you do. You took care of Holly after Justin died, didn't you? Isn't that what your marriage was all about? You said you didn't love her. You just did what you thought was right."

God, he hated it when she turned everything around to be about him. He hadn't even let counseling go as far as to unearth his feelings of guilt over Justin's death. Maybe marrying Holly *had* been penance. Maybe he had tried to make up for her losing Justin. Just like he'd tried to make it up to his dad.

And then he'd had to make it up to Jamie for his mother leaving.

"You're a giving, caring man," Ryanne said, her voice gentle. "It's who you are. And it's one of the things I appreciate the most about you. But I don't want to be taken care of. And I don't want to be one of your projects. You don't have to feel sorry for me."

"I don't feel sorry for you. Why should I?"

She glanced away. "I don't know."

"I told you I love you. Doesn't that mean anything to you, either?" They shouldn't be standing feet apart in his garage when he told her this—he should be kissing her, holding her. Their entire relationship had been ill-timed, and this was an ideal example.

"If you truly do love me, Nick, then it's the best gift I could ever hope to receive." She placed both palms over her heart. "I'm honored. But I can't stay and let you fix my life."

"I'm not Mason," he said, still trying to convince her. "I won't hurt you."

"No." She shook her head and dropped her hands

to her sides, as if frustrated by trying to make him understand. "I just can't stay."

And she was gone.

Nick spent the following hours going over the things that had been said, digesting the truth Ryanne had served up and forced him to swallow. His guilt over Justin's death had been at the root of much of his stress, he admitted. He had blamed himself for not doing more, for not going along that night that Justin had asked him to accompany him—the night he had died.

Was he his brother's keeper? He had thought so. And he had tried to make up for failing him by marrying Holly, by taking the sheriff job, by making his dad's life easier. His own wants and wishes had been shoved to a back burner, where they only got stirred when time allowed.

He wanted Ryanne, but she had her mind made up to move to Albany. He didn't know of anything he could do to change that. He had tried, played his trump card and lost. He couldn't make her love him back, and he would have to spend the rest of his life missing her.

He wanted to expand his custom car business, but being the sheriff took all his time. He didn't need the money, but the county needed him.

How many times had he thought that and stayed with the job, anyway?

The county could find someone else. Duane or Bryce could move up to the senior position. Elmwood, all of Crawford County, would go on as it had for a hundred years—and he didn't have to be the sheriff. He would have more time with Jamie, something else he wanted.

A sad-sweet ache made his chest feel hollow. He would never have Ryanne.

From Nick's back deck, Ryanne and Jamie watched Lisa Crenshaw show the Whitaker house to a well-dressed young couple. The woman was quite obviously pregnant.

"They gonna buy your house?" Jamie asked.

"I don't know." The prospective buyers had stayed inside for half an hour, then come out to look around the yard and see the garage. "Their van won't fit in that old garage," Ryanne said.

"Nope. They could build a new one like my dad did."

"Yes, but your dad also updated the outside of your house, so that it all blends together. A new garage would be an eyesore behind my house."

"What's an eyesore?"

"Something that doesn't look pleasing."

"Oh. Like when Benny Perkins threw up at Sunday school?" Jamie made a face. "Didn't look too pleasin' on our worktable."

"Exactly," she agreed.

She pretended to be absorbed in Jamie's Hot Wheels puzzle on the round glass table when the Realtor looked over and pointed her out to the prospective buyers.

Several minutes later Lisa Crenshaw walked over. The van at the curb was gone. "They loved it!" she said.

"Did they?" Ryanne stood and moved to the wooden railing.

"They plan to turn the bedroom on this side into a nursery and knock out a doorway in the wall between. The husband would like to take out those built-in cabinets in the dining room and put in sliding glass doors that open out to a hot tub in a garden area."

"But those beveled glass doors are authentic to the house!"

"You know these young people," she said with a dismissive wave. "They don't appreciate the quality and dignity of turn of the century architecture."

"Then they should find a new house—with modern embellishments."

"It won't be your house anymore," Lisa said with a grin. "What will you care? You'll have your money. The full asking price, I'm betting."

Ryanne's stomach squeezed into a knot.

"Say, you're not having second thoughts, are you?"

Biting her lip, Ryanne shook her head. She listened to the woman's assurances that she'd call her as soon as she had an offer, and watched her return to her car.

"That piece goes here," Jamie said.

"Oh." Ryanne had been holding a puzzle part for the past five minutes, lost in troubled thoughts. She worked the cardboard cutout in and pressed it down.

"Good job," he said. "That *was* a tough one."

Nick came home soon after, and they exchanged a few stilted pleasantries before she excused herself and went home.

Staring at the beautiful leaded glass cabinets, she imagined the new owners taking them out and replacing them with sleek sliding glass doors and an eyesore of a hot tub. Why, that would look like—like Benny Perkin's throw-up!

Disgusted, Ryanne made herself a sandwich and did a load of laundry. *She was going to have to let go.*

Throughout the evening, she looked around and mentally released each piece of furniture and each fixture. She'd told Nick he was always trying to make other people happy and not pleasing himself, but she had issues of her own to work through. The beautiful California condo hadn't really pleased her; the red Viper had been surprisingly easy to let go. Parting with all the things she'd once considered so important paled beside leaving this house for good—and the thought of leaving Nick and Jamie was even worse.

Days like today had shown her that spending an hour watching an anthill or throwing rocks in the creek was time well spent for her peace of mind and contentment. Jamie had taken her back to her days of carefree youth, reminded her of the good things she'd never appreciated.

Nick had shown her that people were more important than promotions and raises. Jobs and possessions would never give her the sense of worth she sought. Unconsciously she'd been coveting a place where she really mattered; she'd been seeking self-respect, looking for someone who would love her unconditionally.

Nick had given her all that and more. And she'd thrown it all back at him.

Lightning arced downward, splitting the night sky with radiance, then disappearing. Ryanne stood on her front porch and watched the vivid, ethereal light show. Thunder shook the panes of the leaded window behind her. A startlingly cool breeze whipped her hair and spat a few cold drops of rain on her arms and face. She went inside to shut off lights and the window units, then gathered a pillow and a crocheted afghan and snuggled into the creaky porch swing to watch the storm.

Even with the wind and lightning raging on all sides, she felt no fear in this place, and she realized she had always felt safe here. Her thoughts traveled to Albany, a city she'd only visited, felt no special affinity for, yet planned to make her home. The cost of living was definitely higher than here. There were reports of layoffs, so how secure would her position be?

With no seniority in the company, she could lose her job and have nothing on which to fall back. Nowhere to come back to. Because this safe place would be gone.

Leaving wasn't what she really wanted to do. And now she knew it. But unless a miracle happened, she was locked into this course of action.

Sometime during the night, Ryanne moved from the damp swing to the couch in the living room. The phone woke her early the next morning.

"Ryanne! We've sold the Viper! Where do you want the money sent?"

Forrest Perry's excited voice shook the last shreds of sleep from her brain. Was this her miracle? "Just like that? No haggling over the price?"

"Nope. You get exactly what you asked and I get

a healthy commission. Thank you for the business. Just let me know where to have the funds deposited.''

''Wait.'' Ryanne dug her Franklin from a drawer in the dining room and read him the number for her depleted savings account. She thanked him and hung up. A twist of good fortune at last!

A new feeling of hope welled inside her. This would pacify the IRS for at least another six months, and considerably lower the payments. She flipped through her phone book, called the contact person with whom she'd been dealing, and identified herself.

After the agent took her identification number and found her account, she said, ''I'm making a substantial payment this week. What can we do to make arrangements for the balance?''

Later, Ryanne sang in the shower, dressed and made another call. ''Lisa? This is Ryanne Davidson. I've changed my mind. I don't want to sell the house.''

The Realtor was silent a moment. ''You're staying in Elmwood?''

The decision slid into place in that moment. Ryanne didn't want to go to Albany. She didn't want to establish herself all over again in the cutthroat advertising business. She wanted to stay. ''Yes. I'm staying. Can I get out of the listing agreement?''

Over the phone, Ryanne could hear paper ripping.

''Hear that? I'm sorry to lose a client, but pleased as punch to have you for a new neighbor. That's the papers you signed. They're in the trash.''

''Thank you, Lisa. Thank you.''

Ryanne ran across the soggy ground to the house next door, hoping to be in time for Jamie when he woke. Knocking, she entered the kitchen. Nick's coffee smelled delicious; she poured herself a cup and took a sip.

She felt more than heard Nick's presence behind her, and turned slowly. He stood in the doorway, dressed in casual slacks and a knit pullover, holding a mug.

The sight caught her off guard. "Where's your uniform?"

"In my closet."

"You're not going to work?"

"No." He crossed to the coffeemaker and refilled his cup.

"Is everything okay?"

When he turned back to her, she noted how he hesitated for a moment, then said, "As okay as it's going to get."

Footsteps pattered down the stairs and Jamie shot into the room. "Hey, Rye!"

"Hey, big guy."

The boy plopped onto a seat in the cushioned nook. "What would you like for breakfast?" she asked.

"Just orange juice. Dad's takin' me to the Waggin' Tongue for buffalo pancakes!"

"Oh." Suddenly, she felt very much like an outsider. Nick hadn't bothered to call to let her know he wouldn't be needing her to stay with Jamie. That was odd.

"Dad's taking a vacation," Jamie added. "Aren't you, Dad?"

Nick nodded.

"You could have let me know," she said, hurt and probably not covering it up well.

"I didn't know myself," he replied.

"He put in his renegation," Jamie added.

"His what?"

"Resignation," Nick corrected.

Ryanne's attention riveted on Nick in surprise. "You're resigning?"

He nodded.

"From the county?"

He nodded again. Leaning a hip against the counter, he looked into his mug and then at her. "You said a lot of things that made sense. I was trying to make up for Justin's death in all the ways you pointed out." He glanced at Jamie, and she understood he was talking about marrying Holly, as well as the sheriff's job. "I'm going to do some things I want to do now."

"Expand your business?" she asked, excited for him.

He nodded and set down his cup. "And take some vacation time before school starts. I'm shopping for land for offices and a showroom. Jamie and I are going to fly to Disney World."

Ryanne couldn't have been more surprised. Or more pleased. Jamie would be thrilled to have more time with his father. And Nick deserved to live out his own life without trying to please and take care of everyone else. But her sense of alienation also intensified. Nick and Jamie had each other—and Mel.

She had...well, she had a chance to start over, too.

"Dad, look!" Jamie shouted.

He had pulled back the curtain and was sitting on his knees in the seat, staring out the window.

"What are you looking at now?" Nick asked.

"The sign! The house-seller lady is taking down the sign!"

Nick leaned over his son and looked out the window.

Lisa Crenshaw hadn't lost any time getting out to remove the For Sale sign, Ryanne thought gratefully.

Slowly, Nick straightened. Jamie let the curtain fall back. Two sets of vivid blue eyes turned accusingly on Ryanne.

"Those people who want a hot tub bought your house," Jamie said, dejection wilting his formerly exuberant posture.

"The house sold," Nick echoed.

Ryanne studied the hurt in their eyes, her recent impression of estrangement dissipating in the realization that they both loved her and were crushed at the thought of her leaving.

She shook her head. "No," she managed to say.

"They didn't buy it?" Jamie asked. "Then who did?"

"No one did. I changed my mind. I'm not going to Albany. I'm staying."

Jamie let out a whoop, but Nick simply stared at her.

"I never understood Elmwood before," she said, hoping to explain. "I never appreciated it, never understood that the people really care about each other. I wanted to leave for all the wrong reasons. I thought job status and financial success would give me the fulfillment I was looking for. But they didn't.

"And then," she continued, "pride carried me further than I ever should have gone. Pride kept me from being entirely honest with you about my financial and marital situation, too.''

Nick found his voice. ''Jamie, go wake up your grandpa.''

Jamie scurried toward the hall that led to Mel's room. ''I'm gonna tell him the good news!''

When they were alone, Ryanne let the last manacles of pride and embarrassment fall from her shoulders like a heavy mantle. She took a deep breath. ''Mason was never faithful to me.''

Nick's eyes revealed his empathy. ''I'm sorry, Rye.''

''That's the least of it. He never paid taxes, either. By the time I got wise, he had funneled all of the company accounts into his own pocket, eradicating any hope of turning things around, and disappeared. The debt I owe is to the IRS. I sold everything I owned, but it was only enough to hold them off for a while.''

''Disappeared?''

''I spent five hundred dollars a day for a private investigator, until there was nothing left. If the government can't find Mason, I don't have a prayer.''

''But you are divorced?''

She nodded. ''I divorced him after I found out about the women...but before I learned about the company.''

''You could have told me,'' Nick said.

''You would have wanted to help.''

He shrugged. ''I wouldn't have thought less of you.''

''No, I guess you wouldn't have. But there you

have it. The whole ugly truth. And the reason I came back here. I thought I was a failure.''

"So this is why you thought I'd feel sorry for you.''

"Yes.''

"And pride is what kept you from letting me help.''

The word came out with greater difficulty this time. "Y-yes. Can you forgive me?''

"There's nothing to forgive, Rye. In fact, I have a lot to thank you for.''

"You do?''

He nodded and took a few steps closer. "Your confidence and ability to dream big dreams are the perfect counterbalance for old steadfast Nick, don't you think?''

She shrugged, but smiled at his bright outlook.

"I need you to challenge me,'' he said.

"That's never a problem, is it?'' When he reached for her hand, she almost cried with happiness. He still wanted her.

"I guess success is being fulfilled at whatever you love to do,'' he said, and touched her cheek. "I'm going to expand my restoration business. What would you love to do?''

"I thought about that all night,'' she said, enthusiasm returning to her voice. "I think I'd like to try my hand at buying and selling furniture and collectibles. Do you think Elmwood is ready for an antique shop?''

"You'd be great at that.'' His eyes twinkled with hope and happiness. "Anything else you'd like to try?''

"Like what?"

"You had another offer recently. Have you forgotten?"

His proposal, of course. And she'd jumped to the conclusion that he was just trying to take care of her.

"That's an important position, Nick."

"You bet it is."

"I'd expect a signing bonus."

Amusement turned up one side of his incredibly kissable mouth. "Such as?"

"Such as a loan to pay off the IRS, so I can avoid the killer compounding interest."

"You'd let me?"

"I would pay you back."

He pulled her into his arms and she went eagerly. "We could work that out." He kissed her with all the love and devotion he had to offer, with the same hope and expectancy she was feeling. The happiness she'd sought for so long had been right next door—and she'd been too foolish to realize it.

"Where will we live?" Nick asked, one eyebrow raised in question.

"My house would make a good showplace for an antique shop…and I'd be living right here beside it."

"See, Grampa!" Jamie shouted behind her. "I told ya she's staying! And my dad's kissing her again!"

As though he regretted the untimely interruption, Nick ended the kiss, but gazed into her eyes and smiled. "That's not all, Jamie. I'm going to marry her, too!"

"Whoopee!"

"Now we can all go have buffalo pancakes together!"

Ryanne wasn't sure whose shout was louder, Jamie's or Mel's. But Nick's laughter was definitely the most resonating. He threw back his head and laughed, and she joined him. Jamie and Mel enveloped them, and teary hugs were exchanged.

That night Ryanne left Nick while she ran to the house and packed a few more belongings. She would need a suitcase for the trip to Florida, where she and Nick would be married.

Placing items in her carry-on, she thought over the day, over all that had transpired and the plans they'd made so joyfully. She'd never been so filled with peace and contentment. She was going to have a family. A family who loved her. A family she loved.

A realization struck her hard. Nick had taken a risk by declaring his love for her when he wasn't assured of her returning the feelings. And even though he'd proposed and she'd accepted—even though she loved him from the depths of her heart—she had never told him.

He was upstairs in his room now, waiting for her. Ryanne turned and rummaged through her nightstand drawer, found the flashlight and switched off the lamp.

Nick stood at the window in the room where he'd spent so many lonely, sleepless nights, watching the house next door, the house where the girl he'd loved all his life had grown up. Only a few months ago, he would never have believed that all his most sacred and secret dreams would come to pass over this sultry summer, and that he'd be changing his entire life and marrying Ryanne.

He wouldn't even have dared to imagine he would be able to sleep the oblivious sleep of a guilt-free man. Perhaps tonight he would....

The light in Ryanne's bedroom window was extinguished and he watched, ready to follow her movements as she returned to him.

Instead, a light flashed from her window. Another. A series of flashes. Puzzled, Nick leaned against the window frame and concentrated. Dots and dashes, that's what they were. He wracked his memory for the Morse code alphabet he and Ryanne had learned one childhood summer many years ago.

On the second go-round, he interpreted the simple message: *I love you.*

Nick's heart stopped for a full minute, then chugged to an energetic pace. He moved to the wall switch, flipped the light on and off in the same coded message, then left it off and ran down the stairs and through the house.

She met him at the edge of the moonlit garden, the cadence of locusts and the scent of tomatoes the backdrop for her breathlessly spoken declaration. She pressed herself into his embrace and hugged him with all her being. "I love you, Nick Sinclair. I love you."

* * * * *

▼ SILHOUETTE®
SPECIAL EDITION™

AVAILABLE FROM 18TH JULY 2003

THE ROYAL MacALLISTER Joan Elliott Pickart

The Baby Bet: MacAllister's Gifts

For two weeks only, Alice MacAllister and irreverent royal Brent Bardow could laugh, love and ignore the future they'd never have. But she couldn't help wondering what it would be like to be his royal bride…

HIS EXECUTIVE SWEETHEART Christine Rimmer

The Sons of Caitlin Bravo

Celia Tuttle knew that falling madly in love with her boss, Aaron Bravo, was a terrible mistake—she *knew* he'd never marry. Offering her resignation was clearly the solution…but would he let her go?

TALL, DARK AND DIFFICULT Patricia Coughlin

After his accident, daring pilot Major Hollis 'Griff' Griffin no longer cared about anything—except perhaps delectable Rose Davenport. Could she break down the icy barriers around Griff's heart?

WHITE DOVE'S PROMISE Stella Bagwell

The Coltons

Handsome playboy Jared Colton was the town hero, but single mother Kerry was immune to his charm. Rescuing her child caught her attention…but what would he do to keep it?

DRIVE ME WILD Elizabeth Harbison

Grace Bowes' first job interview *ever* was with brooding bachelor Luke Stewart, the man who'd once made her heart beat madly—before she'd married someone else. The man who still made her wonder: what if…?

UNDERCOVER HONEYMOON Leigh Greenwood

Maggie Oliver had an undercover assignment, a pretend honeymoon— with CIA agent Noah Brant, the man who'd once been her lover. Could this deadly charade lead them back to the love they'd lost?

0703/23a

Maitland Maternity

Where the luckiest babies are born!

Cassidy's Kids
by Tara Taylor Quinn

Troublesome twins… A single father…
An old flame…

Sloan Cassidy is a single dad with eighteen-month-old twins and he needs help! He knows one person who could help him, somebody he would love to see again. The trouble is, he hasn't been in touch with her for ten years...

Ellie Maitland has always had a soft spot for children and Sloan's little girls. But everyone knows this gorgeous rancher broke her heart. Everyone that is, except Sloan!

4 FREE

books and a surprise gift!

We would like to take this opportunity to thank you for reading this Silhouette® book by offering you the chance to take FOUR more specially selected titles from the Special Edition™ series absolutely FREE! We're also making this offer to introduce you to the benefits of the Reader Service™—

- ★ FREE home delivery
- ★ FREE gifts and competitions
- ★ FREE monthly Newsletter
- ★ Exclusive Reader Service discount
- ★ Books available before they're in the shops

Accepting these FREE books and gift places you under no obligation to buy, you may cancel at any time, even after receiving your free shipment. Simply complete your details below and return the entire page to the address below. *You don't even need a stamp!*

YES! Please send me 4 free Special Edition books and a surprise gift. I understand that unless you hear from me, I will receive 6 superb new titles every month for just £2.90 each, postage and packing free. I am under no obligation to purchase any books and may cancel my subscription at any time. The free books and gift will be mine to keep in any case.

E3ZEE

Ms/Mrs/Miss/Mr ....Initials....................................
BLOCK CAPITALS PLEASE

Surname ....

Address ....

....

....Postcode...............................

Send this whole page to:
UK: FREEPOST CN81, Croydon, CR9 3WZ
EIRE: PO Box 4546, Kilcock, County Kildare (stamp required)